DRUGSTORE in Another World

~ The Slow Life of a ~ Cheat Pharmacist

NOVEL
1

WRITTEN BY
Kennoji

ILLUSTRATED BY
Matsuuni

Airship

Seven Seas Entertainment

TRANSLATION: Elliot Ryouga
ADAPTATION: Kat Adler
LOGO DESIGN: George Panella
COVER DESIGN: Hanase Qi
INTERIOR LAYOUT & DESIGN: Clay Gardner
PROOFREADER: Kelly Lorraine Andrews, Linda Lombardi
LIGHT NOVEL EDITOR: Rebecca Scoble
PREPRESS TECHNICIAN: Rhiannon Rasmussen-Silverstein
PRODUCTION MANAGER: Lissa Pattillo
MANAGING EDITOR: Julie Davis
ASSOCIATE PUBLISHER: Adam Arnold
PUBLISHER: Jason DeAngelis

ISBN: 978-1-64827-414-5
Printed in Canada
First Printing: May 2021
10 9 8 7 6 5 4 3 2 1

A Brand New World's Medicine Making

*U*GH, I'M SO DONE with work. *I just wanna skip it till the end of time.*

That was what I thought to myself as I made my way toward my workplace.

Suddenly, I found myself in the middle of a forest.

"Er...where am I...?"

This is weird. A second earlier, I'd been in the business district, surrounded by office buildings. Now, I was ringed by trees. I even heard the cries of unknown animals.

Glancing downward, I saw not asphalt, but dirt and fallen leaves. Nature stretched out beneath my feet.

Am I dreaming? I wondered. *Don't tell me I got so sick and tired of work that I'm seeing things...? That's gotta be it.*

I tried punching myself. *Smack!*

"Ow!" I immediately regretted assuming that, since this was all a dream, the blow would be painless. "What the hell?!"

Wait, I thought. *That means this forest's real?*

I heard a strange shriek. "Meoink!" Following the cry, I spotted a pig mewing like a feline.

"Is that weird creature a pig, or a cat?" I furrowed my brow, staring at it until a sentence appeared in my mind's eye.

MEOWPIG: Catlike hog. Staple ingredient in many dishes.

Hunh, I thought. *Was that a status screen or something? I've never seen anything like it before.*

I reflected on the strange animal, unfamiliar trees, and the fact that the city I'd been walking through had suddenly transformed. "Don't tell me I'm in another world...?"

Indeed, it seemed like I was in a completely different place.

"SWEET!" I pumped my fist victoriously. *No more worrying about oversleeping, no more crowded trains, no more crappy job. Goodbye to all that junk!*

I mean, what else was I supposed to think? It wasn't like I came here of my own free will. I had no clue how to get back; it was totally out of my hands. *Even if I did know, I wouldn't try.*

"Whoa, now," I muttered. "It's a little early for celebrating."

Overconfidence would've been reckless, since I was deep in the forest. I could easily imagine bumping into monsters or dangerous beasts.

"Grrrrrrrrrrr..."

Yikes! My shoulders hunched. I'd just heard some beastly growl; where had it come from? *Man, already? Isn't it too early for an enemy encounter? Wait...it's pretty common for protagonists to have useful skills for situations like this.*

Concentrating on myself, I looked at my status.

KIRIO REIJI: Otherworlder. Twenty-four years old.

Hoping for an impressive skill, I read the final line.

SKILLS: Identification, Medicine Making

That's it? No magic? No abilities I can use to fight? I couldn't help feeling bummed as I cautiously observed my surroundings.

The growl I'd heard moments earlier repeated. Now that I really listened carefully, the creature sounded as though it was in pain. I was so surprised when I first heard it that I hadn't realized.

I gingerly peeked into the thicket where the terrifying snarl came from, only to see a large white wolf lying on the ground. The beast's eyes were closed in pain; blood ran from its open wounds, covering its white fur.

Had it gotten caught in some sort of trap? Did someone take it down? I had no way of knowing.

"Hey, are you okay?" In response to my voice, the wolf slowly opened its eyes, but soon closed them again. "Jeez, don't I have anything? Medicine, or..."

Sure, it wasn't my responsibility to save some random animal I just stumbled upon, but I didn't want to leave it to die. I rummaged through my bag, but nothing in there could've helped.

I glanced at the old bag the wolf lay on. Since it was wrapped around the creature's shoulders, it must've belonged to the wolf itself.

"Sorry about this." I pulled the bag from under the animal.

Inside, I found a small bottle the size of my index finger. It contained some strange blue-green liquid.

POTION (REGULAR): Stops blood loss. Effective on superficial injuries.

"A potion!" Those things typically healed HP.

I immediately uncorked the bottle and brought it toward the wolf's mouth. Its nose quivered a bit and its eyes widened.

"G-grr...?!" The wolf seemed less surprised by my presence than by the strange fluid I held in front of it.

"You had this potion on you. Say 'ahhh'!"

I urged the wolf to open its mouth, but I don't think the attempt at communication worked. It turned its head, then stretched its tail toward me and tried to swipe the bottle out of my hand.

"Whoa! Close one." I barely pulled away in time. "Hey, c'mon now. This belongs to you, pal."

How would a wolf even ingest this on its own? I wondered. *Well, whatever. Maybe it distrusts me because I'm human? It might think I'm trying to feed it something dangerous. In that case, I should drink some in front of the wolf to prove that it's safe.*

I brought the bottle to my mouth and caught a whiff of the liquid. "Yuck! What the hell?! This smells like crap!"

Otherworldly potions smell shockingly like garbage!

My survival instincts screamed at me; I gently closed the bottle. "Yeah, I get why you're against drinking this junk."

Supposedly, good medicine tasted bitter, but this potion just stank. *I'd never wanna put this stuff in my mouth.* Its horrific aroma lingered even after I closed the bottle. Frankly, it smelled so bad that it kind of crossed over into being funny.

So, it turns out otherworldly potions are laughably smelly. What exactly is this horrific smell, anyhow? It was like someone had soaked a dishrag with spoiled milk and raw sewage.

While playing RPGs, I definitely made characters drink potions if they were in a pinch health-wise. *Jeez. I bet they hated that.*

If I ever found myself in a video-game world, I'd definitely designate a character I didn't use in combat the "potion carrier" and make them carry the main party's potions. Nobody would want to be within five meters of them.

As I imagined this hilarious scenario, the wolf's tail swept the potion out of my hand and onto the ground.

"Ah, crud. You gotta drink this, buddy," I sighed. "What're we gonna do? I get that it smells awful, but..."

"Grrr..." The white wolf rasped.

At this rate, this creature's not gonna last long. As I observed the animal sadly, I recalled something important. *Right! I have a medicine-making skill. Maybe I can heal the wolf with that?*

"Hang in there, pal," I said before searching my surroundings, although I knew that the beast probably didn't understand my words.

Medicine making, I thought. *I can't imagine that's anything but literal, right? Luckily, I'm in the middle of a forest. There should be all kinds of herbs and nuts I can use to make medicine.*

I began identifying the flowers, weeds, and trees growing nearby. "Bingo!" I picked all kinds of unfamiliar plants and harvested their roots and leaves, gathering a bunch of resources that could prove useful.

I'd be lying if I said I wasn't concerned about combining all the ingredients, considering that I could barely cook. Thankfully, the medicine-making skill apparently included "refinery," which meant that I naturally knew what I needed to do.

I mulched the roots, stems, and leaves, then mixed them into the bottle of water in my bag. All that was left was to close the cap and shake the bottle. *Is this really going to work?*

Despite my apprehension, the water inside began to glow slightly.

MINERAL WATER -> POTION (EXCELLENT): Stops blood loss. Highly effective on superficial injuries.

"It's done!"

The mixture was translucent, with a slight green tint. *It actually sorta looks like a sports drink.* I glanced over at the weakened wolf, only to find that it was looking back at me.

Wait. Actually, it's looking at the water bottle in my hand.

The creature rushed over and balanced on its hind legs, its eyes sparkling. "Grrr!"

"You can stand on two legs?!"

Distracting me with its agility, the wolf snatched the bottle out of my hand and thirstily downed the fluid. *Hunh. It can hold the bottle in its paws.*

"Grrrrrgh…" Seemingly remembering its leg injury, the wolf sat.

It's not whimpering anymore, either. Maybe the pain's gone? I sighed in relief. I hadn't thought that creating a potion would be so simple. Even someone with no innate knowledge or background in pharmaceuticals could mix a basic one. *This medicine-making skill's something else, man.*

Since I also had the identification skill, I could immediately tell that making the potion had worked. I sipped it, curious how it tasted. "Hrm."

It's actually pretty good!

It was a teeny bit sweet, with a refreshing aftertaste. "Wait...I've drunk this before! The flavor's the same as that one sports drink!" This realization stunned me.

Meanwhile, the wolf slowly rose to all four—not just two—legs. "Are you okay now?" I asked.

Obviously, it didn't respond. Instead, the wolf circled me and pounced onto my knees. It was so big, I couldn't help getting knocked over.

"Grrrgh!" The wolf quietly growled above me.

Its body glowed, and before my very eyes, its fur disappeared and its muzzle shrank. The white wolf morphed into a silver-haired young girl with wolf ears, a tail, and fangs.

"Huh? A girl...?" I glanced at her status.

> WEREWOLF: Type of demihuman. Can take a human or wolf form.

So, you're telling me she was a werewolf this whole time? I always figured they were more vicious. I guess not.

The werewolf girl's blue eyes stared straight at me. "Noela say thanks. Many thanks. Almost dead."

Noela swished her tail back and forth as she spoke.

"Er, you're welcome..."

"What that?" she asked. "Very tasty."

"This? It's a potion." Without listening to a word I said, the beast girl crept up and sniffed me. "Wh-whoa! You're way too close!" She pinned my shoulders to the ground, peering at me, and began to lick my lips. "H-hey! Stop that! What the heck?!"

Panicked, I tried to escape from beneath Noela, but failed. *She's way too strong! I totally underestimated her!*

She paid me no mind whatsoever. "Very tasty! Mouth very tasty!"

What in the world is she talking about? I'm down here freaking out, and she's just licking me! What is she, some kind of kiss monster?!

"Hey, seriously!" I exclaimed. "Gah—stop that!"

Jeez. I only just arrived in this strange world, and a beast girl's already tackled and licked me.

"Tasty, tasty! Very tasty."

I guess she thinks I taste good. Oh—she must be licking my mouth to taste the potion I sipped!

"Stop for a sec!" I ordered. "See this? It's the potion—er...the, uh, 'tasty-tasty'—from earlier!"

I pointed at the bottle on the ground. Noela immediately pounced on it. *Clank, clank!*

She struggled with opening it, of course. "Grrr..." Her ears drooped sadly.

"C'mon, give it here." I stood, grabbed the bottle, and unscrewed the cap for the girl.

As soon as I handed it back, she downed the liquid. *Since it's a potion, you're not really supposed to chug it, but whatever.* All I could do was grin, since Noela at least looked like she was enjoying it.

"Just a heads-up—that's medicinal," I warned her. "At any rate, I'm glad you feel better."

"Tasty, tasty! Super tasty."

"I was shocked when you came at me on your back legs," I added.

"Hm?" Noela shook her head. "Noela can't stand up when wolf."

So, she'd done it without realizing. "Hey, I'm gonna head into town or somewhere. I guess this is goodbye, Noela."

"Noela go too! Follow Master!" she exclaimed.

"Er, pardon?"

Noela nodded emphatically and pointed at me. "Master save Noela! Noela repay!"

"You mean repay *me?* I think that's over the top."

I hadn't saved Noela to get her to pay me back. To be honest, though, it'd be helpful having someone like her guide me through this unknown world.

Noela repeated her intentions in a broken sentence: "Noela go with!"

She seemed dead set on this. "All right," I said. "In that case, I appreciate the company!"

I stuck my hand out. Noela grabbed it and squeezed it happily with both hands, tail wagging.

She's less like a wolf and more like a puppy, I decided. "I hate to spring this on you already, but do you know where the closest town is, Noela? Could you take me there?"

My hand still in hers, Noela began to walk. "Master, follow!"

And so, my otherworldly life with the werewolf girl began.

20

2

The Potion Revolution

AS WE TROTTED through the woods, I asked Noela tons of questions.

"So, uh, that was your potion, right? Why didn't you drink it?"

"It stink. No good. First time bought. Brought with me."

In other words, she bought it without knowing what it was. *Hunh.*

According to Noela, a battle between mankind and the Demon King's subjects had erupted worldwide. However, our location—the Est region's Kingdom of Granad—was supposedly about as far as one could get from the war's front lines. Noela had only recently arrived from her town near the battlegrounds, and there was little danger of the demons coming here.

Since I only possessed identification and item-creation skills, that seemed perfect, as far as I was concerned. I'd only just arrived in this strange new world; it would've been a bummer to have to worry about the demon armies threatening my life.

Noela held my hand and guided me this whole time. Suddenly, her ears twitched. "This way."

"Hey...so, uh, can you tell whether monsters and stuff are nearby?"

"Mm-hmm." Noela seemed to frown for a moment.

I patted her head gently, grateful for her help. She was much shorter than me—probably about 150 centimeters tall, if that. However, she was much larger as a wolf. *Man, werewolves are fascinating.*

We continued through the woods, eventually making our way to a proper road.

"So, what happened to you?" I asked Noela. "Why'd you collapse like that? Did someone attack you?"

"Suddenly injured. Ran away."

It was a little hard following her broken speech. Still, I at least parsed that Noela had headed into the woods to look for food, come across a strong monster, and just barely gotten away with her life. Since the enemy attacked her suddenly, it must've evaded her senses.

The village we were headed toward, Kalta, finally came

into view. It was far smaller than a city, and was more like a one-horse town in the middle of nowhere. According to Noela, she visited Kalta fairly often. Not for work or anything like that, just for day-to-day stuff.

As we entered Kalta, I heard a cute sound next to me.

"Master. Tummy rumble." Noela professed her hunger shamelessly.

"No kidding."

I'd have loved to grab a bite myself, but I had no money to speak of. *Well, maybe if I sell that potion I made, I'll earn some fast cash.*

I had Noela lead me to a general store and headed over to the manager.

"Welcome!" the man said cordially. "Haven't seen you around these parts before. Are you a traveler, lad?"

I concisely explained our circumstances. "Erm, that's about the gist of it. I'd love to sell one of my homemade potions. Think you can take a look?"

"Oh, homemade potions, you say? That'd be a huge help," the manager replied. "We've been out of 'em for a while now. We sold our stock to the military."

"But aren't we far away from the front lines?"

"That's exactly why we sold them, young man. A tiny town in the boondocks doesn't need potions if the Demon King's army ain't coming around."

He might be right, but what if someone got hurt? They'd need potions.

"Even if we make 'em ourselves," the manager added, "nobody buys 'em much, so they end up overpriced."

That made sense. I pulled a bottle from my bag and presented it to the manager.

"Tasty, tasty!" Noela's eyes glimmered as she pointed at the bottle.

"What's this, lad? The *potion*?" asked the manager skeptically.

"Is there something strange about it? What do normal potions usually look like?" I'd seen the potion Noela carried, but it was entirely possible that hers was unusual.

"Hold on," said the manager, rummaging beneath the counter. "This one here ain't for sale. I keep it in case of emergency."

POTION (REGULAR): Stops blood loss. Effective on superficial injuries.

Quietly, I picked up the manager's potion bottle. *Hrm. That's the same as Noela's, all right.* I slowly brought it toward her nose; she responded by impulsively fleeing the general store.

"Master, that no good! Stinky. Hate!" Noela shook her head as she peeked in from outside.

The older man frowned at us and shook his head. He must've thought we were ignorant or something. "What're you saying? All potions are like this. They're bitter, gross, and stinky. That's just how it is."

"The laundry's still not done?" a woman cried. "Dear, what're you up to?! Come here!"

"Ah, sorry, love! I'm helping a customer! I'll deal with that laundry later," the manager replied. He turned to me, grinning. "Pardon me. My wife can be difficult sometimes."

"Get your butt over here!"

His wife's loud voice made the manager jump. He turned to face me again.

"Hey, it's fine," I told him. "I'm in no rush."

"Ha ha! Apologies."

He disappeared into the back. It wasn't long before I heard loud noises and voices come from where he'd vanished to.

"I always tell you, you're not making enough money!"

"I-I'm *sorry*!"

Hell hath no fury like a wife scorned.

Noela came back inside; she crouched behind me, ready to brawl. "Sense battle. Noela protect Master." She was simultaneously stalwart and adorable.

The manager finally returned with a tired grin, leaning against the counter and shaking his head. He was clearly trying to act relaxed, but he looked like he'd seen a ghost, and his nose was bleeding.

"Ah, perfect timing," I said, offering him my home-made potion. "Here, try drinking some of this. Trust me."

"Young man, I hate to tell you, but I'm not a potion fan. They don't agree with me. Plus, they stink." Despite the manager's posturing earlier, even he steered clear.

Noela repeated her opinion. "Tasty, tasty!"

That persuaded the manager to cautiously pick up the bottle. He shut his eyes tight before taking a swig.

"Ah! This is great! Wh-what is this stuff?" he asked with trembling hands. He set the bottle down. "It's delicious!"

He looked at me as if I were some kind of monster, teeth chattering. The color returned to his face, and his nosebleed stopped. *I guess "excellent" potions are a cut above the rest.*

"A-a potion that tastes good? I-Impossible! I-It's a breakthrough!"

"Whoa, now. You don't have to exaggerate."

Noela shook her head. "Noela's master amazing! Breakthrough! Potion tasty-tasty!"

"It's delectable and easy to drink!" the manager added. "Lad, if this ain't a breakthrough, I don't know what is."

This dude's seriously getting worked up. I made the thing, and yet he was the one celebrating.

Suddenly, the manager bowed so quickly, he slammed his head onto the counter. *Smack!*

"I'm begging you, lad, let my store sell your potions!"

"Yeah, of course," I replied. "That's why I came here to begin with."

"I know, I know. Selling such a revolutionary product at a local general store is a waste. But please!" the manager continued.

"Listen to me for a sec! Look, it's fine," I repeated. "Seriously. I'm happy to sell you these."

"Please! We just had our fifth kid, and the family finances are in the red. I might have to shut this store down. Please, sell us your breakthrough potions! Let's start this revolution together!"

He was really down for the "revolution." Almost too much, actually. "How many bottles do you want?" The nasty "regular" potions came in fairly small containers. *If that's the standard size, I should be able to make quite a few.*

"I'll put them in these and sell them, if you..." the manager paused. "Wait, are you sure?"

"Master say okay. You not listen," Noela pointed out.

"Th-thank you so much! What's your name, lad? I need the name of this revolution's hero!"

"Kirio Reiji. You can call me Reiji."

We exchanged a firm handshake. "The revolutionary hero Reiji," chuckled the manager. "Rolls right off the tongue. Heh heh!"

Buddy, could you please let go of my hand?

I began pouring my homemade potion into the manager's small containers. My bottle wasn't full, since Noela drank some earlier, but it still held more than enough liquid to fill twenty-five smaller vials.

According to the manager, regular potions sold for about ten thousand rin. *I wonder how much that is in yen?*

Seeing me puzzled, he explained. "If you want to stay overnight at the local inn, for example, it runs you five thousand rin. Lunch costs about six hundred."

Doesn't seem all that different from yen, actually.

"I'm gonna start advertising this 'tasty-tasty' potion's effectiveness!" declared the manager.

"Oh, before you do that—we should sell this breakthrough potion a little more cheaply than normal potions," I suggested. "That'll make it easier for customers to impulse-buy. It'll help word of mouth."

"Whoa! Spoken like a true revolutionary!"

We decided to sell the first twenty-five potions for eight thousand rin each, which was under the standard market price. However, I'd receive about two thousand rin per bottle.

Just like that, I'd earned myself fifty thousand rin! Now, I wouldn't have to worry about food or shelter for the next few days.

The manager ran out to advertise his new product, leaving his wife in charge of the general store. She came over to Noela and me. "Sorry about my hubby."

Noela crouched behind me. "Master protect. Protect Noela."

I patted her head, shooting a smile at the manager's wife. "I'm sure these potions will sell."

"You have our thanks."

After chatting with her for a bit, Noela and I exited the store. The manager had kind of gone crazy with excitement, but I would've been lying if I said it didn't feel good to be appreciated like that.

Noela and I ended up going to a big dining hall she frequented, and the two of us grabbed a bite to eat.

The menu was full of all kinds of strange characters, but mysteriously, I had no problem reading any of them. I'd been worried that the dining hall would serve weird foods, but much to my surprise, the menu contained easy-to-eat dishes like teriyaki, pickles, and so on. I could even order soup and bread.

Eventually, Noela and I left the restaurant in search of an inn. Then we heard a ruckus coming from the general store.

What's going on?

We peeked inside, only to discover men filling the store. I saw farmer-looking dudes, lumberjack types, and lightly armored soldiers—all sorts of people who'd be in danger of getting hurt at work.

"One per person!" the manager's wife yelled out.

A young soldier exited the store, tilting his head at the potion in his hand. "What a weird-colored potion. I bought one because she said it'd be easy to drink, but... Let's see, here." He sipped it. "Whoa! What is this stuff?!"

The young soldier looked as though his eyes were about to pop out of his head. "This is a potion?!" he exclaimed. "For real?! It doesn't taste like fresh trash!"

Noela simply nodded in quiet agreement.

So, that's what regular potions taste like. Man, I'm glad I never gave them a try. What kind of recipe would you have to follow to make something flavored like that?

The folks who tasted my homemade potions while leaving the store all trembled on the spot at its flavor.

"This is revolutionary!"

"This potion's starting a revolution!"

"This is such a breakthrough, it's a downright revolution!"

Man, these guys really like the word "revolution," huh? I was pretty sure that the potions would work as my skill described, though, so I wasn't too worried about "revolution" being hyperbole.

Finally, the manager came and expressed his gratitude. "Thank you so much, lad! I knew this revolutionary potion would sell! Think you could make some more? Folks are asking, and, well..."

"Sure," I replied. "I'll bring them over tomorrow."

"Thank you!" the older man replied, beaming.

If I sold the potions directly to customers, I could've made a lot more profit, but it wasn't like my goal was to get rich. I just needed enough money to be comfortable.

"Do you know where you're spending the night, lad? Would you like to stay with me and my lot? My house can get a bit rowdy, but I'd love to thank you for all you've done."

"We'll grab a room at an inn, since I have money from the potions," I replied. "But thanks! I appreciate the thought."

And so, Noela and I parted ways with the manager. Since we were two complete strangers to him until today, his willingness to put us up overnight meant that he had a good heart. I hoped this would all work out for him.

"Master, what wrong? Say something?"

"Nah, it's nothing."

With a lightness to my step, I began searching for an inn, and my first day in another world came to a close.

3

Making Potions

BACK AT THE GENERAL STORE, before setting off for the woods, I got myself a mortar and pestle, a basket for medicinal herbs, a small knife, and ten bottles. I tried to pay for all this, but the manager would have none of it.

"If I took money from you, Reiji my lad, the old lady would be furious."

I decided to let it go for now.

Noela was currently in wolf form, howling and wandering around near the village. That was apparently how she detected dangerous monsters and beasts nearby. Granted, I had no clue whether there was any real meaning behind her noises.

I, on the other hand, was harvesting medicinal herbs and the like for tasty potions. I hadn't noticed yesterday, since I was so thunderstruck, but herbs had become easier to spot. It was almost like they stuck out from their background. The stalk of the "aero" plant, a medicinal herb known as "torigisou," and last but not least, a therapeutic root called "amane"—one by one, I collected them and stuffed them into my basket.

"This should be more than enough," I told myself, my basket now full.

At that point, Noela finally got back, her body shining as she returned to her human form. "Master ready?"

"Not quite. I was hoping you could guide me to a river or something. Any water source, really."

"This way."

Noela led me to a cobbled trail next to a stream. The visibility was great; it would be easy to tell if a monster or wild animal approached. The water itself was clean and transparent. According to my identification skill, it was perfectly suitable for medicine.

"Noela help Master!"

"Thanks a ton. Think you can grab me some water?"

Noela nodded. Holding a bottle to her chest, she headed to the stream. Her tail wagged happily as she knelt and began to fill the bottle.

Meanwhile, I ground the herbs I'd just collected with the mortar and pestle I got earlier. I squeezed the plants nice and tight against the mortar's surface, grinding out all the juice.

Noela came back with the bottle of water in hand. I poured in the ground flora, capped the bottle, and began to shake it. Immediately, the mixture reacted the way it had when I'd tried this yesterday; it glowed faintly and turned the color of a sports drink.

> **POTION (EXCELLENT):** Stops blood loss. Highly effective on superficial injuries.

"Perfect. It worked."

"Tasty, tasty! Tasty, tasty!" Noela reached for the bottle.

I pulled it away from her. "Hold your horses. Don't get riled up. I'll make you some later, okay?"

"Will wait."

"Good girl."

I ended up mixing an extra potion and giving it to Noela. Her tail wagged slowly as she gulped down the drink. "Arrroooo!"

I continued my work, bottling ten potions before eventually heading back to Kalta.

◆◆◆

As Noela and I walked through town, I couldn't help but notice more people around, many of whom whispered amongst themselves.

"Yo, is that the so-called revolutionary hero?"

"I heard he has black hair and a beastling serving him. That's gotta be him!"

Er, did I do something wrong? I wondered.

"Noela not beastling. Werewolf," Noela complained.

The general store manager, Alf, stared at us wide-eyed as I explained today's delivery. "So, uh, I ended up making quite a few potions. I filled the ten bottles you gave me."

"A-are you kidding?! That's enough for a hundred sales!" he exclaimed. "You filled them all that quickly?!"

Oh, right. Each of Alf's bottles held about ten retail potions, I remembered. "Quickly? I mean, I've been working since this morning, and it's already noon."

The manager's eyes bugged out dramatically. "That's breakneck fast!"

I suppose I have no clue how long mixing potions normally takes.

"I-I knew it," he continued. "As a genius alchemist expatriate—er, a revolutionary hero—you're one of a kind."

"So, you're the guy starting the weird rumors," I replied.

I entered the store with the manager, and we transferred the potions to smaller bottles. Noela had already drunk her fill of the stuff on the way home; still, she stared longingly at my hands as I poured the potions.

"Reiji, my lad, most craftsmen struggle to mix a hundred potions a month," the manager informed me. "For slower potion-makers, even sixty can be rough."

"Hunh. They sure take it easy."

"I'm not talking about how *much* they work. Grinding herbs, drying them, all of that—it takes time. You should know that better than I."

"Wh-whoa! Wait a sec," I said. "Of course I know that! I, uh, was just testing you, Alf! Y-yeah, totally."

"Master sweaty."

"Quiet, Noela."

"Woof."

A hundred potions per month, on the high end. If that was really the case, my medicine-making skill was practically magic.

Which means Alf wasn't really off the mark calling me an "alchemist." Hrm. The war on the front lines had ravaged Kalta's potion supply, so potions were hard to come by here in the boondocks.

If magic existed in this world, there must be healing spells, but I hadn't seen any yet. Without a healer present, people had to rely on potions. I had experience with that—in video games, anyway.

The manager lined a store shelf with bottles of the breakthrough potion. He removed the "Sold Out" sign, replacing it with one reading "Revolutionary Potions Available."

"Hey, Reiji my lad, have you had lunch yet?" he asked me. "C'mon, eat with my family."

"I'll gladly take you up on that offer. Thank you very much."

That was how Alf's wife ended up making me and Noela lunch. We both indulged in warm soup and crusty bread, only to spot a small group of children in the dining room entrance, staring at Noela fiercely. Alf's kids, no doubt.

"Beast lady!"

"Her tail looks super-duper soft!"

"Look! Look! Her ears are moving and stuff!"

"She's sooooo cute!"

Noela looked at me with a troubled expression. "Master. Master. Watching me."

Maybe she's embarrassed. "Yup, they sure are."

One after another, the kids came into the dining room and began petting Noela all over.

"Her tail's so soft!"

"Her fur's so smooth!"

"Her ears! I'm gonna touch her ears!"

Noela looked as if she were about to cry. "Master. Master. Touching me."

"Yup, they sure are."

Teary-eyed, Noela resisted the children's play. "Don't pull!" They didn't seem to pay her any mind.

Alf's wife smiled, a baby in her arms. "I'm so sorry about the little ones."

"No, no. You treated us to such a wonderful lunch, after all. No harm done."

"Master no speak for Noela!"

Even from the dining room, I could tell things had gotten loud in the general store. "One per person!" I heard Alf shout.

Looks like business is booming yet again today.

"Thank you so much, Reiji," Alf's wife continued.

I returned the smile she gave me. "Please, I honestly did nothing. Your husband's paid me more than enough for the potions. And, hey, we all gotta look out for one another."

As the children continued to roughhouse, Noela pulled my cuff. "Master! Master! Pwease, save meee!"

"Sorry. As a wolf girl, it's your fate to be snuggled to death," I chuckled. *Life is full of trials and tribulations, Noela.*

Still, I felt a little bad for her, so I made her a potion later.

40

4

Buying a House

EVERY MORNING for the past week, I'd sold home-made potions to the general store. After doing that over and over, I found myself with healthy savings: three million rin, to be precise.

Frankly, I spent every day nervous that someone would rob me. Three million in a week was crazy, right? The fact that I'd made that much meant that Alf, the manager over at the general store, made even more.

According to him, his wife didn't get angry about money anymore.

Folks from other towns heard rumors about Kalta's "revolutionary" potion and started visiting to try it, so it still sold quickly. Recently, locals even started treating the potion like a premium beverage, buying it just because they enjoyed the flavor.

Since I made money continually from the potions, I approached Alf with an important proposition.

"You know, I don't wanna keep staying at the inn. I'd love to live in a proper house, if possible," I explained. "Are any for sale around here? I wouldn't even mind renting, though I'd like to buy one, if I can."

"Hrm, let's see. There's *one* house for sale, but it's kinda…" Alf beat around the bush. "Nobody even knows who owns the place anymore. It's so old and busted, folks were thinking about just knocking it down."

"I don't mind."

Noela nodded. "Master and Noela's house!"

It didn't seem as if she cared much whether the house was old or new.

"What's up, young man?" Alf asked. "This seems kind of sudden."

"Well, I'd like to create medicine in a proper lab. Plus, I was thinking of opening my own shop."

With my medicine-making skill, I could produce all kinds of treatments. I was sure I could craft medicine this world had never seen before, as long as I had the ingredients. I'd help the townsfolk, make a bit of money on the side, and live comfortably. I just had the feeling that that lifestyle suited me best.

I honestly expected Alf to be against the idea, but instead, he grinned at me.

"Sounds great! As a man, you gotta aim to be lord of your own domain, right?" He patted me warmly on the back.

"Are you sure it's all right for me to sell potions on my own?"

"What the heck are you babbling about? You mixed the breakthrough potions to begin with, Reiji, my lad. You can do whatever you want with them!"

Looking at the general store's potion sales, you could've described me as a golden goose. Yet Alf had no issue letting me go solo. He'd treated me to lunch, taught me all kinds of things about this world, and been a huge help since I'd arrived.

"I'm gonna keep selling your potions," Alf added. "The general store's will be the same price as yours."

"Ha ha! You're a lifesaver."

Alf patted my back once again. Then, leaving the store to his wife, he showed us to the house he'd mentioned. As we drew close to the property, I immediately noticed that there were fewer and fewer people around.

"This is it," Alf said.

"It's boarded up."

"As I said, this is it."

"Er...but it's boarded up."

"I told you it was so bad that folks considered demolishing it, didn't I?"

I was tongue-tied. This small, one-story building was way worse than I could ever have imagined. I wouldn't have been terribly shocked if a gust of wind blew it over like a poorly-constructed popsicle-stick house.

"Since nobody knows who owns this dang place, it's just sat here for years," Alf added. "The only reason it wasn't knocked down is, well..." he coughed. "Anyhow, it's completely free."

"For some reason, the words 'there's no such thing as a free lunch' just came to mind," I replied.

Does some mysterious monster live in there or something? Back in my old world, the place probably would've been a hotspot for punks.

"Just, uh, be careful, okay?" Alf left with those mysterious words, making his way back toward the general store.

"Be careful"? Hunh.

"Master, inside! Hurry!" Noela pulled my hand.

Fine. We can take a look, and if things seem really bad, that's that.

Much to my surprise, the only thing that made a weird noise when we entered was the door itself.

Sure, the place is dusty, but the construction's pretty solid. And if something's busted, we can just hire a carpenter, I reflected.

"What do you say we make this our new home?"

The werewolf girl was clearly game, her eyes sparkling with excitement. "Noela live here with Master!"

That meant we had cleaning to do; there was no way we could live here as is. I attempted to buy some cleaning supplies from the general store, but the manager didn't charge me for it. *Dammit, Alf. You're never gonna let me pay for anything, are you?*

Noela and I returned to our house—formerly condemned—with a broom, a dustpan, and rags. It took us about two hours to finish cleaning the place. Sure, it wasn't sparkling, but it was definitely way better than it had been when we got there.

"This place is old, but it's a legit house," I admitted.

It didn't take me long to pick a room as my official laboratory. I sprawled on the floor, my arms and legs outstretched.

That was when I first noticed the young lady stuck to the ceiling.

I'll just go ahead and describe exactly what transpired.

"Um...so, I've been watching you for a while now," she said, meeting my eyes. "I have a question. Are you this house's new owner?"

I hesitated. *There's a blue-eyed blonde girl stuck to the ceiling! She's pretty cute, too. Gah—what am I even thinking?!*

"You're quite skilled with a broom!" she added.

Now she's complimenting me?!

"Uh...d-do you mind my asking who you are?" I stammered.

"Oh, gosh, pardon me! My name's Mina."

"N-nice to meet you. I'm Reiji."

"I'll have to throw you a housewarming party, Mr. Reiji!" Mina smiled brightly.

W-well, jeez, ain't she just the gosh-darn cutest!

I was so flustered that my internal voice morphed into something odd. Ignorant of that fact, the girl on the ceiling clapped her hands together merrily.

"U-um, e-excuse me—uh, can I ask you a question?" I inquired. *Is it really okay to question her? Isn't this a situation I should try to overlook? No, I'm way too curious for that.*

"Tee hee! Of course!"

Man, she's energetic. "So, uh, are you fond of—you know—ceilings?"

"I've never been asked that before."

Nobody's asked?! Seriously?! What were *people asking, in that case?!*

"But, well, I suppose so."

"I-I figured," I said. "Otherwise, why would you be on the ceiling, right?"

"Precisely. This is all part of the job!"

J-job?! There's a job that just requires you to dangle from a ceiling, looking at stuff?!

Noela trotted over, her hands on her stomach. "Master, hungry."

"Oh, yeah, sure. Noela..." I pointed at the ceiling girl, Mina. "Could you look at the ceiling for me real quick?"

Noela tilted her head. "What wrong, Master? Something on ceiling?"

"Huh? Er, yeah. A girl."

"Hmm? No girl."

"For real...?"

"For real."

W-well, gracious, ain't she a real live ghost! My internal voice was still odd.

Unaware, Mina straightened proudly. "Hee hee! As long as I don't use my special power, only this house's master can see me."

Is that something to be proud of?! Now, I totally understood why Alf told me earlier to be careful.

"I figure that, as long as the house's master sees me," Mina added, "it's fine if the whole family can't."

"I-Is that so?" I replied.

I told Noela to go eat at Alf's place. She rushed out, leaving the house quiet.

"You sure like lying on the floor!" Mina said.

"Er, well, how else could I talk to someone on the ceiling?" I paused, then asked the big question. "Are you a ghost?"

"How rude! I'm no ghost."

Whoops. It sounded like I'd stepped on a landmine. *Sh-she's gonna haunt me.* Really, though, Mina didn't seem like she planned to take revenge. Instead, she pouted cutely.

"Then what are you?" I continued. "Noela couldn't see you."

"Well, I lived in this house a hundred years ago."

"In our society, we call someone like that a ghost."

"I told you already, I'm not a ghost! I stay here on the ceiling and watch over people who move in, ensuring they live happy lives!"

"Nobody asked you to do that." Even though it seemed like she meant well, that sounded extremely invasive.

"Still, it's so strange," Mina continued. "Whenever I make eye contact with a new homeowner, they turn white and pretend they don't see me."

"Why am I not surprised?! I totally get where they're coming from!" I exclaimed.

"Did something give them all stomachaches?"

"Isn't it obvious?! The answer's closer than you think!"

"Most people leave the house after a few days without my getting to chat with them. It's been forty years since there was an owner, Mr. Reiji. That's why I'm so happy I got to meet you." Still clinging to the ceiling, Mina smiled.

"How do I get you to disappear?"

"I *won't* disappear!" Mina turned away. "Don't treat me like some ghost."

"If you're not a ghost, what are you?"

"Let's see," she mused. "Nobody's ever asked me that before, so I don't have an exact answer. If I had to explain myself, though, I'd say that I'm this house's *protective deity*!"

Mina's expression announced that she considered that a perfect description.

I imagine this "protective deity" led to the sad situation where nobody wants to live here. "So, how do I get you to go away?" I repeated.

"I won't! Why're you being such a big meanie, Mr. Reiji? Why do you keep saying such sad things?"

I'm the "sad" one here. I just arrived in a brand new world, and now I'm talking to a ghost! Maybe I should rephrase the question.

"What do you want, Mina?" I asked. If I could grant her wishes, she wouldn't have lingering regrets, and maybe she'd pass on to the next life.

"What do I want? Um...I just want the residents here to lead happy lives."

"Noela and I just have to lead happy lives?" I repeated.

"That would certainly satisfy me." Mina flashed me a smile as bright and warm as the sun outside.

The problem was, "happy lives" brought me back to my original request that Mina leave. *That'd be the fastest way to make me and Noela happy, right?* Still, it didn't look like that'd happen anytime soon. *Well, whatever.*

"I guess I'll get ready to open the shop, then," I concluded.

"Oh! I'd love to help!" Mina left the ceiling, landing gently on the floor.

"You can do that?!" I cried.

"When I descend, I can't keep an eye on you anymore, so my job—"

"Yeah, yeah, your cushy job just watching from the ceiling. I get it."

"Hey! That's mean, Mr. Reiji!"

"Is it?"

"You could act nicer, at least! You're going to hurt my feelings!" Mina stuck her tongue out angrily. Then her expression changed entirely. "Mr. Reiji?"

"Yeah?"

She flashed me the brightest grin I could imagine. "I'm having a lot of fun right now."

"Is that right? Good for you."

The house was old and haunted, but I renovated it into a drugstore nonetheless.

5

The Hopped-Up Carpenters

I DROPPED A DECENT CHUNK of change hiring some carpenters in town to remodel part of the house as a storefront.

Clank. Clank. Rumble. Rumble. Clank. Clank.

All sorts of sounds came from the house's entrance. According to the carpenters, it wouldn't take too long—about a week or so—to wrap up their renovations.

I was busy formulating new medicines in the laboratory when Mina appeared with three teacups. "The tea's ready, Mr. Reiji!"

"Much obliged."

Noela, meanwhile, inspected my work curiously. When Mina entered, the young werewolf's ears perked up. She turned to face the ghost; then she turned back to me, poking my side.

"Master. Master. Strange girl here."

"Well, duh. Wait—can you see her?"

Noela nodded vigorously.

"Oh, that's right!" Mina said, grinning. "Mr. Reiji, I forgot to mention this. Since I didn't use my special powers for years, I can stay in this physical form for ages!" She poured tea into the brand-new cups I just bought.

"Noela, this girl here is Mina. She's apparently a ghost," I explained.

"Okay," replied Noela.

That didn't take much.

"Allow me to prove it to you!" Mina exclaimed. "Woosh! I bet you can't see me anymore, Miss Noela!"

Noela hesitated. "She gone?!"

Mina was actually still right there, but I guess Noela couldn't see her.

"How's this?" Mina reappeared.

"She back."

"Or this?"

"Only arms. Weird."

As Mina and Noela played, I left to check up on the carpenters. I didn't need a whole lot of space for the drugstore, so I couldn't imagine that the renovation would be too much work. Despite that, it didn't look like the carpenters had made much progress.

"Um, how's it going?" I asked. They glanced up at me.

One—Mr. Gaston—rose to his feet. "I-It's exactly as it looks, M-Mr. Pharmacist."

Mr. Gaston was the town's veteran carpenter; he was over eighty. *Hell of a long life.* Although I said he "rose to his feet," I should add that he was hunched over; his face only reached my waist.

Mr. Gaston grimaced a little. His eyes seemed buried in wrinkles. *This guy's pretty old,* I mused, *but the other carpenters respect him like some kind of legend. Hope he doesn't hurt himself. Gah...now I'm worried.*

I decided I shouldn't say anything, since worrying about a pro like Mr. Gaston might be rude. The other carpenters with him were elderly, too. The youngest of the bunch was in his sixties!

Pointing his trembling finger at various spots, Mr. Gaston explained the situation to me.

"So, you're saying it's gonna be difficult to wrap up in a week?" I asked.

"Say wha...? I can't hear ya!"

"A week! Isn't! Enough! Time! For the renovation?!"

"Aye!" Mr. Gaston replied. "Way back in the day, the old lady was all—"

I wasn't asking about your old lady!

"Right, right!" interjected another carpenter. "Then he got cheated on!"

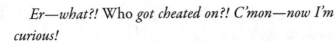

Er—what?! Who *got cheated on?!* C'mon—now I'm curious!

Mr. Gaston continued to blather leisurely. "Look, it's exactly what ya think. I can't move around like I used to, so things'll take a bit longer than expected, Mr. Pharmacist. That's how my night of trouble with the old lady started!"

"Uh, you're mixing work up with private details!" I replied. "Wait...could I hear about this 'night of trouble'?" *Seriously, I have to know.*

"We get tired real fast, got it?" Mr. Gaston replied. "Everyone's gotten so old."

"Which is why work doesn't fly by like it used to!"

The other elderly carpenters chimed in to explain. Up till now, they'd done jobs like this on their own. I couldn't imagine the frustration they must've felt at being unable to do what they'd trained for.

"We're mighty grateful to ya, Mr. Pharmacist," Mr. Gaston concluded. "Ya made us townsfolk all them potions—potions that sold out across the region! Better yet, they taste delicious! Now, we can work without worrying about getting hurt."

The other carpenters nodded.

"That's why we wanna help ya out as best we can," added Mr. Gaston. "Still, there's no triumph over old age!"

They get tired fast, huh? Isn't there some kind of treatment to help them get past that exhaustion, even just momentarily? Wait... Since I can mix potions, maybe I can make that?

"Hey, don't push yourselves too hard," I told the carpenters, then headed back to my laboratory. I flipped through the pages of the plant encyclopedia I'd bought.

"Master okay?"

"Yeah. I just wanna make something."

I could picture the finished product, and instinctively knew what ingredients I needed. *This medicine-making skill sure is useful.*

There were no plant photos in the book, unlike encyclopedias in my old world, but I at least got the species' names and whereabouts. *Looks like I can find all these herbs in this area.*

"Your tea's gone cold, Mr. Reiji. Would you like me to pour you another cup?" Mina offered.

"Thanks, but I'm actually heading out."

"Is that so? Take care!"

"Will do. Watch over the place while I'm gone."

"Righto!" Mina exclaimed cheerfully.

I prepared my toolkit and left. Noela's enemy-detection ability was tremendously useful, so I had her tag along, and we set out toward the usual forest.

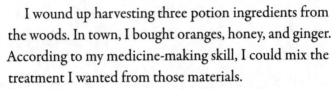

I wound up harvesting three potion ingredients from the woods. In town, I bought oranges, honey, and ginger. According to my medicine-making skill, I could mix the treatment I wanted from those materials.

With the goods in hand, I locked myself away in my laboratory.

Before long, Mina poked her head in. "Welcome home, Mr. Reiji, Noela. What would you like for lunch?"

"Don't worry," I replied. "I'll eat later."

Noela's tail wagged; she focused on my work with great curiosity. "Noela eat later, too."

"Gosh. You both need to make sure you have lunch. I'll make you something quick."

Mina headed for the kitchen, whistling happily. To my surprise, she was pretty considerate.

I crushed and dried the potion ingredients, then mixed them with orange and ginger juice, adding a little honey.

"What make, Master?"

"Hey now, I can't go ruining the surprise. Could you bottle some water for me?"

Noela trotted off to do as I asked, returning quickly. Thanking her, I poured the blended juice into the bottle, then capped and shook it.

Splash! Splash! Splash! The liquid glowed as usual.

> **ENERGY POTION:** Relieves exhaustion. Functions as stimulant. Effects vary person to person.

"It's done!" I told Noela.

"Done? Done?"

I sipped the liquid. "Mm-mmm!"

"What is it? What is it, Master?"

I just wanna tell someone—anyone—that this tastes like my favorite energy drink! It sucks that it's not carbonated, but it's delicious enough as is!

"Noela try too!"

"If you're not used to this stuff, the flavor might startle you. Take a small sip, okay?"

I poured a bit of the energy potion into an open bottle. When Noela tried it, her fur stood on end so quickly, I swore I could hear it. Her wide eyes looked back and forth.

"Hmm...?! Master amazing! Tasty, tasty! Noela feel like can fly!"

"Please don't try."

Noela ran in circles, eventually sliding between my legs and climbing my back in an attempt to soar. *She's hyper.*

At that point, Mina arrived with a plate of food. "I made some sandwiches, Mr. Reiji! This way, you can work while you eat." Her eyes widened as she spotted Noela running amok.

"Thanks a lot, Mina. I'll definitely eat those soon. Could you do me a favor and watch Noela for a sec?"

"Of course. What's wrong with her?"

"She's got too much energy." I bit into the ham-and-veggie sandwich. *Yeah, this is good stuff.*

"Hunh." Mina tilted her head.

I poured some of the energy potion into five smaller vials, then headed to where the carpenters were working.

"Here. For each of you." I handed one bottle to each old man.

They curiously inspected the contents, bringing the bottles close to their faces before lowering them. *Ah. Their vision must not be great.*

"What's this weird liquid?" Mr. Gaston asked, speaking for all the carpenters.

"Let's just call it a drink that'll energize you guys," I replied. "It's not guaranteed to work, so I guess it's more accurate to say you'll hopefully *feel* more energetic."

"Hrmph." Mr. Gaston chugged the bottle, then froze in place, making a strange sound. "Hwaa—?!"

"How is it?" I asked. "It might be an acquired taste, but it should relieve your exhaustion and wake you up a bit. The results'll vary by person, but..."

Mr. Gaston trembled as he took a step, his hunch gradually lessening until he stood up straight.

"Are you evolving?" I chuckled. "Er...now's not the time for jokes. How's your hip, Mr. Gaston?"

Mr. Gaston clearly wasn't listening to a word I said. "This feeling..." he whispered to himself. "Aaaaaaaaah!"

I couldn't help rubbing my eyes. Mr. Gaston was glowing! *What the—?! What's going on?! He's got an aura! Energy's* bursting *from him!*

"I can see it!" he exclaimed. "I can see my youth!"

He suddenly began working with incredible speed. *Clank! Clank! Clank! Bang! Bang! Bang!*

"Wh-whoa," I stammered. "Are you okay?!"

"Silly question! I've never been better! Gah ha ha ha ha!"

"He's like a different person," I gasped. "I can't follow his movements!"

The youngest carpenter, who was in his sixties, patted my shoulder. "What, did you think you saw him just now? That was an afterimage."

"A what?!"

"These moves..." he breathed. "This is the legendary carpenter Gaston at his sharpest!"

"The man I looked up to when I was but a lad," another carpenter agreed. "The legend has returned!"

"Don't just stand there, men!" exclaimed the youngest carpenter. "Bottoms up!"

The rest of the elderly workers gulped their energy potions.

"Er, you shouldn't just chug them like that," I warned.

"Whoa! This job's nothing! We can wrap this up in a heartbeat!"

"Hee hee! The time's finally come to unleash the black dragon sealed in my left hand!"

Their personalities are totally different...and one of them's having some kind of dragon awakening?!

Rumble, rumble, rumble—the elderly carpenters gave it their all. They ultimately finished the renovations that were supposed to take a week in a single day. Instead of working at a steady pace, they just zoomed through the job.

The carpenters had a blast renovating the house. As far as I was concerned, that was the best part. They all told me that they felt young again. And since they finished so quickly, I could open my shop much sooner than I'd anticipated. *Jeez, that energy drink I made worked way too well.*

As the carpenters left, Mr. Gaston turned to me, back straight and tools in hand. "If you ever need more help, just give us a call, pal." He flashed me a grin.

It was a total personality shift. *Too cool.*

6

The Master Archer

AFTER I OPENED THE DRUGSTORE, things got pretty busy for us day to day. I lined the shelves with regular potions and energy drinks I'd mixed. I planned to create more types of medicine, but I was going to wait for requests before I produced them.

Things went surprisingly smoothly. Noela was a huge help, serving as our drugstore's counter girl. On top of that, Mina was great at housework, so she handled everything from cooking to laundry to cleaning. Talk about a talented ghost, right?

Oh, I almost forgot—the store's name. I ended up keeping it simple: Kirio Drugs. I wrote the sign in Japanese, so needless to say, Mina and Noela had no clue what they were looking at.

The drugstore had emptied out for a bit, so I figured it was time to settle down and eat some of the lunch Mina made us.

"Do ghosts have to eat?" I asked her.

"I don't need to, but honestly, I prefer having lunch with everyone."

"They do say meals taste better when you eat with others."

Noela just dug into her food, nodding furiously. I had no idea whether she'd been listening at all.

"Oh, right!" Mina exclaimed. "Mr. Reiji, did you know there's a festival in town today?"

"Whoa. Really?" *Hunh. Now that she brings it up, I did notice that the town was oddly busy.*

"There'll be lots of stalls and events," Mina continued.

"Such as?"

"Well, I believe the biggest one is the long-range archery display."

"Archery display?"

"Mm-hmm. Every year, the elves' most talented archer shoots a target that's super-duper far away—*whoosh*! It's quite amazing."

"That sounds awesome."

I would've been lying if I said I wasn't interested. After all, I hadn't seen a single elf since coming to this world.

They were typically gorgeous, so I thought that I'd love to meet an elf at least once.

A voice came from the storefront. "Pardon me! Is the drugstore manager in?"

I swallowed the food in my mouth and rushed over. "Yes. How can I help y—"

Speak of the devil! The customer was an elf with long ears, just barely shoulder-length blond hair, blue eyes, and a beautiful face. On the elf's back was a longbow, and they wore leather boots.

"Ah, at last," the elf greeted me. "You're the manager? Well, aren't *you* a cute boy?"

"Uh...boy? I'm a grown man. Anyway, how can I help you?"

"Ah, yes. I'm here with a request for the alchemist wunderkind."

"That description's not quite right either. But, well, my potions and energy drinks are over there on the shelf."

"I don't need those. I require direct help."

"Er...what do you mean?"

"My name's Kururu. As you might have surmised, I'm an elf."

"Pleased to meet you. I'm Reiji."

"What a cute name! Ah—I mustn't get sidetracked. I'm out of my element, talking to you!"

"Hunh. Is that so?"

Kururu looked mischievously at me. *He's a guy, right? What's he thinking?*

"It's about the archery exhibition at the festival today," he explained. "I'm the one performing."

"Oh, really? I'm looking forward to seeing that."

Kururu shook his head, clearly disappointed. "I'm happy to hear that, but I've realized there's a chance I might not live up to your expectations!"

I wondered whether this was false modesty—or if that was even a concept in this world.

"Why not?"

"Apparently, my bow's not in the best condition. I can't seem to hit my target."

Can't hit his target? Hold on. The festival's today. "Er... how does that have anything to do with me?"

Kururu flashed me a relieved smile. "I want you to do something about it."

"Practice on your own."

"You're the only one I can count on, Reiji, my dear."

"I'm not your 'dear,' either."

"If you help me out, I promise you can have your way with me!" Kururu giggled, casting me another sidelong glance.

"Do you really think we accept that as payment?"

"What, would you prefer that I *woo* you? Now, don't misunderstand. I'm not saying that's my preference. I just thought it might make you happier. I swear, I'm definitely not at all enticed."

I was an idiot for getting excited about an elf dropping by. "Why ask me? I can't imagine drugstores are the best place to go for this kind of thing."

"I heard rumors of an alchemist who gave Kalta's elders so much energy, it was like they were young again. That's why I thought, if I asked you, your butt might... Er, you might help me hit my target."

At the moment, I couldn't help thinking that he could "target" plenty of other guys. "I guess that's true. But isn't hitting your target a matter of skill?"

"I'd like you to prescribe a treatment that lets me hit my target with complete accuracy!"

"Like hell I can create something like that!" That was getting into magic territory.

"Listen, dear Reiji, I'm completely serious! That's why I want you to give me everything you've got!"

Pounding his chest, Kururu spread his arms wide. *I'm not jumping into your arms, pal.*

"I don't know what to prescribe," I replied. "Are you sure you haven't gotten rusty or something? Could someone else take your place?"

"I'm the forest's best archer. Even if I wanted to decline, nobody could replace me. And, by the way, this definitely isn't a problem with my skills. I've been practicing day and night."

"Fine. I get that a lack of practice didn't cause your problem. But, in that case, why did your skills take a nosedive?"

"That's what I've been asking you!"

"Actually, you've just been hassling me this whole time."

If I don't do something, this elf isn't going to leave. Hrm. He practiced "day and night," but his skills got weaker anyway...?

"Hey, could you be overworking yourself? You know, practicing too much?" Considering what he'd said, that seemed like a reasonable explanation—sometimes over-training could backfire, after all.

I pointed at Kururu. He tried to clasp my hand, but missed. "Ah—so close, yet so far!"

Well, that was close—I don't particularly want this guy holding my hand, I thought. *Wait a sec. I didn't actually dodge his hand; he missed on his own. Aha!*

"Hold on," I said. "Could this be a vision issue? Do you find it hard to see because you're tired?"

"Oh, now that you mention it..."

Focusing on Kururu, I picked up on his abnormal blinking and squinting. *If he'd noticed that earlier, this would've been so much easier. It's my time to shine.*

"You're clearly exhausted. Your eyes are strained," I explained. "Therefore, you can't hit targets at long range."

I was no optometrist, so it wasn't like I could give a full explanation. Based on what I saw and heard from him, however, eyestrain seemed spot on.

"I see," Kururu mumbled. "So, I'm exhausted?"

I glanced at the encyclopedia behind the counter, looking up the ingredients for eye drops. Clean water and salt served as the medication's base, so all that was left was to add shellfish. Luckily, Kururu still had two hours before his archery performance.

"Hang tight," I told him. "I'm gonna whip you up some eye drops."

"Eye drops? Those sound rather *intimate.*"

Jeez, what am I gonna do with this guy?

I left Kururu waiting in the drugstore, heading back to my laboratory. I was already tired; I hadn't expected to deal with such overconfidence today. It would've been nice if he'd stuck to explaining his archery difficulties.

Still munching away at her lunch, Noela looked over. "Customer annoy? Feel better, Master."

"Uh-huh. Thanks, Noela."

She trotted close to me, and I recharged by patting her soft, fluffy head. *Now that I feel a little less irritated, it's time to get to work.* Still, to be perfectly honest, even I found it hard to believe that I could make eye drops with just the ingredients in the encyclopedia.

Mina was drying her hands after finishing some cleaning.

"Mina, there's still some omir shellfish, right?" I figured we should have leftovers.

"We do!" she replied, bringing some over. "Want to snack on them?"

"No. I'm going to use their broth to make medicine."

Mina seemed baffled. "M-medicine?"

I had her boil the shellfish, prepare water and salt, and bring all the ingredients to my laboratory.

Noela was currently flopped over, sleeping. *Time to mix the eye drops.*

I added just a dash of salt to the water. All that was left was to pour in the boiled shellfish broth. I combined the three ingredients in the smallest bottle I had; as usual, the liquid glowed.

> **EYE DROPS:** Effective for eyestrain. Promote cell regeneration.

I'd mixed actual medication with just those three ingredients; anybody with the medicine-making skill could. "At this point, that skill is basically magic," I muttered.

All right, let's try this stuff. I dripped the eye drops into my eyes. "Ah...! Nice and clear."

Heading back to the storefront, I passed the eye drops to Kururu.

"And these are?"

"They're called 'eye drops.' Basically, they'll relieve your eyestrain. One drop per eye. Got it?"

"Hrm."

Drip, drip. Kururu tried them.

Man, I suck at using them myself, but he's really good. I told him to keep his eyes shut for a bit.

"Why?!" he asked. "Don't tell me you're going to steal a kiss?"

"In your dreams." *And stop wiggling around like you're embarrassed.* "All right, that should be long enough. Open up. How do your eyes feel?"

"Huh? My vision's so clear! It's completely different!" exclaimed Kururu, clearly overjoyed. "Reiji, my dear, this is amazing! Thank you so much! I just want to eat you up!"

"Whoa—hey! No eating! Back up." Pushing Kururu's forehead, I held him at arm's length.

"Oh, come now! No need to be shy!"

"I'm not. Personal space, okay?"

"Are you just acting frosty so you can do an about-face later?!"

"Nothing can squash your optimism, huh? If you're happy with the eye drops, get going," I suggested, pushing him away.

All of a sudden, Kururu's expression changed entirely. "I'm going to hit my target for your sake!"

"Aw, man. Earlier, I was so intrigued by this archery event. You're taking the wind out of my sails."

"Catch you later, dear," Kururu left the drugstore, waving.

He wasn't guaranteed to hit his target just because I gave him eye drops, but I was honestly curious. After Noela woke up, I decided to spend some time enjoying the festival before the big archery event. The actual demonstration would be in the center of town, where a fifty-meter-long stretch of land led to a small target. Lots of people already sat in the audience.

When the time finally arrived, Kururu showed up with his longbow. The audience welcomed him with applause and cheers, and the elf responded like a pro. To be honest, it kind of pissed me off how charismatic he was.

Swoosh!

The first arrow glided through the air and struck the target perfectly. As the crowd showered Kururu in heavy applause, he raised his hands.

Once he exited the venue, it didn't take him long to locate me. "This was all thanks to your eye drops! Thank you so much, Reiji, dear." He tried to hug me.

"Whoa!" I dodged swiftly. "Close one. Really, you were skilled to begin with. Eye drops wouldn't help much at that range."

"That's not true at all!" Kururu exclaimed. "I didn't hit the target even once when I was practicing!"

"Well, that's because you ran yourself ragged."

I figured I could at least praise him for working so hard. All in all, Kururu was clearly immensely skilled.

74

7

Fluff Conquers All

ONCE I STOCKED the drugstore with eye drops, they sold particularly well to older men and women. Elderly locals were overjoyed to be able to see their grandchildren's faces; they even came to say thanks in person.

Man, if folks are this pleased with the eye drops, they were totally worth making.

"Um, Mr. Reiji? Do you think you could do some shopping soon?" Mina asked. "We're about to run out of food." Since she was a ghost tied to this house, she couldn't actually leave.

"Oh, sure," I replied. "Do you have a list?"

"Right here."

I grabbed it from her. "Wanna come, Noela?"

"Noela go!"

Shopping basket in hand, we left Mina to watch over the store.

"Take care!" Mina waved to us.

Noela responded in kind. "Yes! Back later!"

With the festival over, Kalta had returned to its normal calm state. *All right, let's see what I gotta grab.*

"What do you think we're buying?" I asked Noela. I opened the list Mina gave me. "Wool underwear?"

Gah! What the heck's she making me buy?! Wait a second—ghosts wear panties? Well, I guess she needs them when she's in a physical body.

"Face red, Master. Okay?"

"Yeah. I'm fine. Hrm...I wonder if she gave me the wrong list?"

Mina was actually quite responsible, but she could be kind of a ditz at times, so it was entirely possible that she'd messed up. Just as I was about to make a U-turn and head back, I heard loud footsteps and a scream.

"H-help meeeeeeee!"

"Wait, wait, wait, wait! Why're you running?! Let's talk! Why, why, why, why—"

As I turned around, I spotted a girl about twenty years old chasing a man around the same age. The young woman held a knife around thirty centimeters long. The man was teary-eyed, while the woman's eyes were bloodshot; she looked positively ghastly.

Nope. Definitely not getting involved. The pair was running in our direction, so I stepped aside to give them space. Instead, they headed right toward me. *Wait, why?!*

When the man and I made eye contact, he looked like he'd found God or something. He ran behind me, taking cover as if I were a shield. "S-save me!"

"No way! Save yourself!"

"I-I'm begging you! Do something about her!"

"What exactly do you expect from me?!"

"Zeral! Why're you running off?!" I heard the girl's voice behind me.

I spun around, shivering and fearful of what I'd find. She immediately thrust the knife toward my throat. *Eeeeeeek!*

"U-um, my name's Reiji," I stammered. "I-I own the pharmacy over there. I have nothing t-to do with any of this."

"You own that drugstore? Ah! You're the alchemist everyone's been talking about! What did you do to my Zeral? You must've given him some kind of weird medication, right? Right? Right? *Right*?!"

Yikes. She seems really out of it—or maybe this is her default state. Zeral trembled behind me silently. *Dude, seriously? No backup here? Noela? No, she's a lost cause.*

Noela was wearing our shopping basket on her head and pretending not to be here.

"I honestly have nothing to do with your Zeral," I told the woman. I turned to the dude behind me. "C'mon, man. Stop hiding and say something."

"Feris is a little sick, okay? Please do something, Mr. Alchemist!"

"I'm healthy, healthy, healthy, healthy! I'm not sick at all! You're the one who's sick, Zeral! What'd you get from this sketchy alchemist?!"

Gaaaaah. They've totally made this my problem.

"Fine, fine. I get it, already," I said reluctantly. "Feris, yeah? Could you please put down the knife? If you don't, there's no way we're gonna fix this mess."

Somehow, my desperate pleas got through to her. She dropped her knife to the ground, then covered her face with both hands and began sobbing.

"I-It's not my fault!" she wept. "Why does everyone make me the villain? Why? Why?"

Okay, yup. She's emotionally unstable. From the outside, it looked less like I'd been roped into a lover's quarrel, and more like I made Feris cry. I grabbed Zeral by the collar. *Yo, stop trying to run away, Zeral.*

"How about explaining this situation to me?" I suggested.

"O-oh, sure."

Folks around us were going about their business, so we relocated to an empty park. I sat Feris down on a bench. Seeing that she was still crying, Noela began to pet her head gently. Instantly, Feris captured Noela in her arms.

"Grrroo?!"

In my peripheral vision, I saw Noela wriggling in Feris's grip. I put some distance between myself and the bench, opting to ask Zeral about the disagreement.

"I'm really sorry about earlier," he said.

"Look, it's fine. What's done is done. But what happened to Feris? No offense, but what's your relationship?"

"Feris and I, well, we recently started dating."

"Hunh. Is that so?" I felt myself getting annoyed. "She seemed really upset. Hell, she's been sobbing. Did you guys get in a fight?"

Zeral shook his head. "No. This happens a lot these days. But today was definitely the worst it's been. I mean, I guess you could describe it as a fight. You see, Feris worries a lot—excessively."

"Hunh." *What else can I say to that?*

"She told me she gets so worried about me, she can't sleep. At first, I thought that was charming, but then it just got worse and worse."

According to Zeral, not only was Feris a worrywart, she was also fairly jealous—scared of being cheated on. Apparently, Zeral buying bread from a female bakery employee was enough to set Feris off.

So, is this the flip side of loving someone too much?

I glanced at Feris; she seemed like she was being healed by Noela's fluffiness. Her expression was blissful, completely different from before. Noela's fluffy fur was truly incredible. *This might be kind of like animal therapy. Fluffiness truly conquers all.*

"I want you to do something, Mr. Reiji," Zeral said.

"You're just gonna dump this all on me, huh?"

"Feris must be possessed! Some kind of demon changed her!" he insisted. "She has a huge victim complex too. She'll go on and on about how I said something that I didn't say at all, or how I *didn't* say something that I definitely did."

"If her worrying is that problematic, why not just break up? You've had enough of this, right?"

Zeral's face immediately paled. He smiled powerlessly. "Want to hear what happened when I suggested we break up, Mr. Reiji?"

"Nah, I'm good." I was sure it had been hellish, if Feris was willing to chase Zeral around town with a knife for lesser crimes.

"That's why I want you to drive away the evil spirit possessing her," Zeral repeated. "Then she'll go back to normal!"

"I'm not an exorcist."

"Oh, right, you're mainly an alchemist."

"You make it sound like I do exorcisms on the side. I don't. I own a pharmacy."

As far as Zeral was concerned, it didn't matter whether I was an exorcist, alchemist, or pharmacist. "Please save Feris! You'll be saving me as well!" He bowed his head deeply.

I sighed in defeat. "Fine. I'll do what I can. But just so you know, if an evil spirit's really possessing her, there's nothing I can do about it."

"Thank you so much!"

The two of us shook hands. I watched Feris playing with Noela; she seemed like an ordinary young woman.

I know I said I'd try to help, but what can I actually do? Medicine won't drive away an evil spirit, assuming she's possessed to begin with. I can't make that call—I should just focus on doing what I can.

"If anything might help...maybe, just maybe..." I trailed off.

"Maybe what?" Zeral asked.

I nodded. "I'm gonna get ready. Come to Kirio Drugs tonight, and I'll give you the prescription then."

"W-wait—you're leaving me alone with her?!"

"She's your girlfriend, isn't she? Buck up, pal. And, hey, she probably isn't possessed or anything." With that, I headed back to the drugstore.

"Ah! Welcome home!" called Mina. "That took quite a while."

"Let's just say I got dragged into some stuff. Oh—here." I passed Mina the paper she'd given me earlier. "I'm guessing you handed me the wrong list?"

Mina's face turned bright red. "O-oh, gosh! I-I'm so sorry! I gave you the wrong one! Eek...!" She pressed herself against the ceiling in embarrassment, covering her face with both hands.

"Wool panties, eh?"

"Please, stop, Mr. Reiji."

I holed up in my laboratory and got started on the treatment. *Crap—I knew I forgot something. I left Noela back at the park,* I realized. *Whatever. I'll leave the animal-therapy gig to her.*

For this, I should be able to use the herbs I picked in the woods and mountains. I ground the dried flowers of a plant I'd gathered, combining the mixture with ginger before bottling and shaking it. It glowed and, bam, medicine complete.

I removed the cap and took a whiff. "Smells great."

After a bit, Noela and Zeral showed up at the drugstore. I handed him the mixture I'd finished earlier, explaining, "It's more like a beverage than medicine, to be honest."

I told him to have Feris drink it before bed. He thanked me and headed home.

Soon after the drugstore opened the next day, Zeral rushed inside.

"Oh. Good morning."

"Morning! Wait, no! Now's not the time for leisurely greetings!" he gripped my hand. "Thank you so much! When I woke up, Feris...she...she was back to normal! She looked so calm!"

"Is that right? Well I'm glad to hear it."

"That medicine exorcised the demon, eh?"

"Not at all. It was just a simple herbal tea."

"Huh? That's it?"

"Yup. Feris told you she couldn't sleep because she was so worried, right? I gave you something to help her insomnia."

> **LANDEN FLOWER TEA:** Effective for nerves. Relaxing. Lowers anxiety/stress.

From the description, I'd thought the tea would have a subtle effect, but it sounded like landen was surprisingly potent.

"It's really easy to flip out over small things when you haven't gotten much sleep," I told Zeral.

The fact that Feris was typically a bundle of nerves anyway had led to disaster. That said, the landen tea did nothing to treat jealousy or habitual worrying. I made sure to inform Zeral of that, and he bowed his head in thanks.

"Zeral, are you almost done?" Feris poked her head into the drugstore.

She and I made eye contact, and she flashed me an apologetic smile. It was just like Zeral said; she looked totally calm, as if the landen tea had washed away whatever possessed her.

"Hang on, I'm coming!" Zeral replied, then turned to me. "See, we're going on a date today."

"Hunh. Is that so?"

Zeral handed me some money and once again thanked me. He turned and left the drugstore with Feris, the two of them holding hands like lovers.

Ah, jeez, c'mon. Now I don't even feel like doing anything anymore. Those dummies should get a room, I brooded. *Eh, whatever. At least nobody died.*

8

An Otherworldly Culture Clash

"**H**ERE, MASTER." Noela pulled my hand as we headed deeper into the woods.

"How much further is this wild plant harvesting spot?" I asked.

"Little more." Wagging her tail, Noela happily trotted full-speed ahead.

She seemed to be in high spirits, at least. She was quite sour after I accidentally left her with Feris the other day. I told her that I'd do anything to make her feel better, so she suggested that I come with her to pick plants in the woods as she always did. Now, here we were.

"Master, look!"

"What's up?"

"This tree sign! Close! Noela find plants nearby."

Before meeting me, Noela came up to this spot almost daily. She'd picked wild plants, then sold them in town or eaten them herself.

Noela stopped in her tracks.

Hrm? Are we here? I used my identification skill to scope out the area, but detected only regular plants—nothing edible.

"Noela?" I glanced at her.

Noela held her nose, her eyes full of tears. "Master, smelly!"

"Huh? Wha...?"

Noela nodded.

Is she talking about me? No...

She pointed at a giant blossom. "Weird. Never seen."

The poisonous-looking flower was about the size of a small child. Its pistil was swollen; without any leaves or stem, it looked like some creepy monstrosity.

> **MORAY FLOWER:** Produces hideous scent only monsters/ beasts can smell.

I inched toward the moray flower, but smelled nothing. "Ah, well. I'm human, so I guess I wouldn't. Can't you just pinch your nose?" I asked Noela, attempting to progress forward.

Noela shook her head. "Eyes hurt a little."

Wow. It's that stinky? I'd heard about particularly intense smells affecting the eyes.

I asked whether there was another route, but Noela told me that the other paths were easy to get lost on, which made them dangerous.

"How about we call it quits for today, then?"

"Grrr...but Noela go together with Master." Her ears drooped sadly.

Noela couldn't go past the moray flower, but she also didn't want this trip with me to have been a waste. *She's such a cutie.*

Since my guide couldn't actually progress, I wasn't sure what my options were. *What should I do?* It would've been pointless to leave her behind. *Hmm. If that flower repels monsters and beasts, maybe I can use it for something later.*

I got close to the moray blossom and put several petals and some pollen in a bottle, closing it tightly.

"Hmm. Oh!" I exclaimed. "How about I make a deodorizer?"

"Grroo?" Noela's ears perked up.

Heading back the way we came, I grabbed some aero and a few other plants and flowers as custom treatment ingredients. Then I headed to the stream we'd used a while ago, plopped down, and started making the deodorizer. The bottle glowed, and the liquid inside turned light green.

> **DEODORIZER FLUID:** Completely removes bad smells.

That description kind of reminds me of a toilet freshener, I mused. "Perfect. It's done. If I put some deodorizer on that flower, it's goodbye stank!"

"No more smell?" asked Noela.

"That's the plan!"

"Garrooo!"

We headed back to the moray blossom; I scooped up some deodorizer liquid with a spoon and splashed it on the plant.

Since I couldn't smell the flower, I had no idea whether the deodorizer worked. I beckoned Noela, and she got close, still pinching her nose.

"Well?" I asked. "Does it still stink?"

"Master! Master! Master! No stink! No stink…!"

"Hey, hey. I got it, okay? Don't pull on my shirt so hard."

Noela's werewolf strength was pretty insane; her pulling at my clothes was basically equivalent to swinging me around.

Facing me with a completely serious expression, Noela took her hand off her nose. It twitched. "Smell really gone."

"Look at you, getting all serious."

With no more obstacles in our way, we finally arrived at the spot where the wild plants were, but...

"Gah!" I yelped. "What the hell?! It stinks here!"

It feels like my nose is gonna fall off! Bleh—my eyes sting! What the hell is this smell?!

I glanced at the werewolf girl, who was humming and pulling up wild plants happily. "Noela, are you...okay?"

What? Is it just me? This whole area stinks!

> BIRUKOSOU: An extremely odorous wild plant. Many avoid its unique taste/aroma. However, some enjoy eating it.

Noela cheerfully picked the birukosou; she had a bunch in her hands.

That's it! And—wait—Noela's eating them like it's no big deal?!

"Got many, Master!"

"Y-you sure have!" *Is this plant sort of like natto? Smelly but tasty? Is that it? I do like natto, but birukosou might be a bit beyond me.*

"Master, take!" Noela sunnily offered me a birukosou plant. "Eat! Master, eat!"

Is she serious? No way, no way, no way, no way, no way. Gah! I-It stinks so bad that I'm about to cry. People in this world eat these? I suddenly empathize with all the foreigners who can't stand natto, I marveled.

"Look, Noela—I'm really sorry, but I can't. It stinks too much, and—"

"Grrooo?! No stink! Wrong!" Noela's expression was now sullen.

Whoops. Looks like that offended her. Guess she must really love this stuff. She did *say she used to come here every day. Wait—what if I use the deodorizer I just made? This birukosou stuff stinks so much, it's affecting my breathing.*

I poured a bit of deodorizer onto the plant.

"Huh? The smell's...gone?" *This stuff is* amazing! *This must be how Noela felt earlier.*

"Master, serious face." The young werewolf girl turned to me and, once again, offered me the wild birukosou.

There's no rule against eating something I used the deodorizer on. It should be fine to consume.

"Master, Master! Tasty, tasty."

"Are you sure?" I closed my eyes and took a small bite.

Crunch, crunch. The birukosou's essence spread through my mouth, and a powerful stench rose through my nose.

Almost immediately, I spat out the plant. "Blegh! Sorry, Noela. This is too much for me."

"Gwwrrr..."

Disappointed that she couldn't share her favorite food with me, Noela slouched sadly. Nonetheless, she continued to pick wild plants.

Man, folks in this world think that stuff's tasty, huh? This might've been the first real shock I'd experienced since arriving. *We all have our likes and dislikes, Noela. I hope you can forgive me.*

Eventually, Noela and I headed back. Mina greeted us. "Welcome home! Ah—I know that aroma."

Inside Noela's small backpack was a load of those wild birukosou plants. To my surprise, the stench didn't seem to bother Mina.

"Hey, Mina. Do you think this stuff's tasty?" I asked.

"Absolutely! And Mikoto said she loves them."

Mikoto was a young girl from a village near Kalta. She sometimes visited the drugstore on errands. Apparently, she'd taught Mina that peeling the birukosou got rid of the vile smell and made it taste better.

"You mean, you don't eat it as is?"

"Of course not, Mr. Reiji," Mina replied. "It smells much too putrid to eat like that."

Is that so? I hadn't even considered that, since Noela

just munched away on the stuff. *If you prepare it properly, it's perfectly edible...?*

For dinner that evening, Mina prepared a dish of the foul plants. I took some of the stir-fried birukosou on the dining table and cautiously brought them to my mouth.

What the hell? This smells kind of appetizing.

"Oh...this is good."

If I'd tried them stir-fried first, I think they would've been too much for me, I mused. *They probably seem delicious because I already experienced the birukosou's gross scent at its full power.*

"Garrooo." Noela had the most victorious look on her face, as if she were saying, "Told you so!"

"I found some strange medicine in your bag, Mr. Reiji," Mina told me.

"Oh, that? It's deodorizer fluid. Just a dash of that stuff erases nasty smells."

"Gosh! You've created yet another product?!" she exclaimed. "In that case, let's leave it in the washroom!"

"Ha ha! I should've known we'd end up using it there," I chuckled. "This world's no different from the last."

Later, I put the deodorizer on the drugstore shelf with the other goods. It ended up selling like crazy to housewives.

9

The Medicine God

NOELA WAS CURRENTLY in the bedroom, napping on my bed; Mina was washing dishes with her back to me.

"Why don't you try this, Mina?"

Soap suds bubbled up everywhere.

"Wah!" she cried. "M-Mr. Reiji! Th-there're so many suds! Save meeee!"

"You used too much dish soap," I told her. "Man, how much *did* you put in there?"

Glancing over at the kitchen sink, I noticed that the bottle I'd given Mina was completely empty. *Yeah, she used* way *too much.*

I'd noticed that Mina took an abnormally long time to do the dishes, so I'd asked her what the deal was. She told me that cleaning up after a meal took about an hour.

I'd double-checked with some of my housewife customers, and they gave me the same answer—so Mina wasn't abnormally slow or anything.

An hour to wash three people's dishes. We eat three meals a day, so that's three hours total...a huge waste of time.

With that in mind, I had Mina try out the dish soap—which led to the soap bubbles overwhelming her. "Aah! Mr. Reiji, this dish soap is super-duper amazing!"

Heh. Right? Right?

"The plates are sparkling white...incredibly smooth!" Mina joyfully stroked a dish's surface.

This should shorten the time it takes to clean a single dish, I thought. When it came to chores, it was important to use one's time wisely. How easily you could do the job was important.

"I haven't even scrubbed this, and it's already so clean," Mina chimed. "It's like magic." She brushed her hand over the faucet, and it poured just the right amount of water. It was controlled by something called a "life stone," which was a common tool in this world. There were multiple kinds, and they all reacted to magical power, which was a combination of physical and spiritual strength. Despite being from another world, even I could use life stones. When you ran a small amount of magic through them, they could do things like produce water, start fires, or turn on lights.

"Dishwashing's going to be much easier now!" Mina exclaimed.

"In that case, this dish soap was worth making," I told her. "I'll go pass on the leftovers to our neighbors."

"See you!"

With several small bottles of dish soap packed in my bag, I headed out. I'd said "neighbors," but really, the buildings nearby were mostly restaurants and such. In other words, they had way more dishes to wash than an average home.

First, I first made my way to the closest pub. A bunch of tough-looking dudes were eating in groups inside.

"Hello!" I said to a girl in the back. I'd seen her around before. "I'm from Kirio Drugs."

"Oh! Um—Mr. Pharmacist!" she replied, as though she'd just remembered me.

That's right! I'm a pharmacist, not an alchemist, or an exorcist, or a revolutionary. Why does it feel like she's the first one to get it right?

"The deodorizer you made has been so useful!" she told me. "I always ran into smells I couldn't get rid of when I was cleaning."

"Glad to hear it works. I actually came today with something new. Would you like to give it a try?"

"What is it?"

"A product that'll make dishwashing much, much easier."

"Wow...!"

I thoroughly described the dish soap to the barmaid, who seemed more than impressed.

As I did so, however, one of the men eating stood up. "Hey, you. You're that guy who's been makin' potions, right? I gotta talk to you about somethin'."

Me? Frankly, when a dude this tough said something like that, I couldn't help but get a little nervous. *I wonder what's up.*

"Doz, cut it out," called the redhaired woman sitting next to the man.

He shook his head. "But, Boss..."

"I'm telling you to cut it out."

Just like that, the big man sat back down.

"Who are they...?" I quietly asked the barmaid.

"The Red Cat Brigade. A mercenary group entrusted with guarding the town, on the lord's orders. The redhead is their captain."

Mercenaries, huh? I gotta imagine they're pretty rough folks. Actually, now that the barmaid mentioned it, I'd seen plenty of these guys standing guard in town before.

The Red Cat Brigade's captain was a ginger-haired beauty with a ponytail and sharp eyes. "Sorry about that, Pharmacist. I know you're in the middle of work."

"Oh, no. It's fine." I bowed my head to her slightly and began to leave.

"Gah! I can't handle this anymore!"

Thump! Thump! Thump! I heard heavy footsteps behind me, and soon after, someone grabbed my shoulders. When I turned around, I found Doz the mercenary standing there.

"Hey, Pharma—no, Mr. Pharmacist. Is there any way you could sell our barracks five potions every day for half price?"

"Er—potions?"

"Yeah." And, just like that, Doz bowed deeply.

Five potions for half price, huh? I'd recently set the potion price at 1,200 rin per bottle. The general store matched the cost. If I sold the Red Cat Brigade that many at half price, it'd be expensive. *Hrm. What should I do here?*

The captain approached, smacking Doz right on the head. "Didn't I tell you to quit blabberin'?"

"But, Boss, your body can't live without those potions no more!"

Er...excuse me? Does she have some curse sapping her life force? Is she drinking potions to cover it up?

The captain scratched her cheek. "C'mon, that ain't true."

"It is! I know it is. Everyone does!"

You're hiding an illness, Captain? You shouldn't worry your men like that.

"Every night, you sneak two potions, don't you?" Doz accused. "On bad nights, you drink five! I count every morning."

The captain clicked her tongue and looked away. "We shouldn't talk 'bout this in the middle of eatin'. Save it for after we go home, and..."

"No, I won't save it! I'll talk 'bout it here and now! Boss, you gotta stop this."

Things had taken an oddly serious turn. The barmaid and I simply watched, concerned.

"You don't drink or gamble, Boss. This is the only thing you ever got addicted to! And we all know that revolutionary potion's addictive as heck. But, at the end of the day, it's medicine! Of course it'll empty your purse if you keep chugging it every night. It ain't cheap! I gotta lay down the law, Boss! Please stop drinking our potions without permission. They're for folks who get injured!"

Crap. This isn't the conversation I expected.

The captain wore a guilty expression; her fingers twirled her ponytail. "I ain't been drinkin' 'em." Her voice was low, like that of a child caught stealing from the cookie jar.

"Stop tryin' to hide the truth! We all know it's you. That's why I'm here tryin' to haggle with the pharmacist, just for you!"

"What belongs to our brigade belongs to me! My stuff's my stuff. Quit whinin'!"

There it was—"Gianism," after the selfish bully character from the famous anime about a time-traveling blue robot cat. *To think that Gian's attitude exists here, too. The main difference is that the captain sounds even more childish.*

The entire brigade piped up, making the captain flinch.

"You know we're havin' money problems lately, right? Who do you think's at fault?"

"Ain't it obvious we ain't gettin' paid enough?!"

"That's *your* doin'!"

According to the Red Cat Brigade members, this was the first time they'd eaten out in quite a while. Since Kalta was in the countryside, I guessed that they weren't paid all that much. Despite that, they'd gotten by...at least, until the captain started downing expensive potions.

I could see why the brigade would be upset. With all that in mind, I decided to interject.

"All right, Doz, I understand," I said. "Every day, I'll make five extra potions and deliver them to the Red Cat Brigade separately. You don't have to pay for them, either."

The mercenaries were astonished.

"Pharmacist..."

"No—he's a god!"

"The pharmacist's a deity?"

"He's a god who's descended to bless us!"

"Psh!" exclaimed the redhead. "It's not like I need 'em or anything, but if you insist, we'll take 'em."

"Don't be like that, Captain! What if you upset the Medicine God?"

"Hmph! I'll cross that bridge when I come to it."

"Oh, Medicine God, we're so sorry! Our captain can be kinda haughty. She's actually thrilled right now."

"I-I ain't haughty, and I ain't thrilled." Her voice was low again.

It looked like I'd gained yet another weird nickname: Medicine God. "Oh...but I do have one request," I added.

These mercenaries served as the town's security force, which meant I could assume that people here generally trusted them.

"When I create new medications, I'm going to give you Red Cat Brigade members the first samples. If you could tell the locals your impressions, that'd be great."

"Is that all? That's no sweat off our backs," the captain said, looking somewhat shocked.

"That's all. Most folks won't want to buy some strange medicine they've never heard of. Even if I tell them its effects, lots of people won't trust it. So, I want you to try my treatments out and offer your opinions to the townsfolk."

At the cost of five potions, I could help out the captain and avoid having to advertise my products. A cheap price, all things considered; a win-win situation.

All the mercenaries but the captain knelt and bowed toward me, repeating, "All hail the Medicine God!"

You guys are starting to look like some sort of weird cult. Please stop.

"Erm…so, uh…I hate to spring a product on you this soon, but…"

We all moved to the tavern's kitchen so I could have the Red Cat Brigade experience the dish soap firsthand.

A few dirty dishes floated in the sink's oily water. "All right, Captain," I said. "Put some of this liquid on a rag, and try to clean a dish."

"S-sure."

Next to her, I had the barmaid wash dishes the way she normally did. As soon as the captain started scrubbing, the sink began to fill with suds.

"Wh-wh-what the heck's goin' on?!" she exclaimed.

"Don't worry. That's just what happens. Please keep going."

"O-okay." The captain continued to wash, her eyes full of surprise.

The rest of the brigade watched intently.

"He's makin' the captain wash dishes?" one muttered. "I feel guilty lookin', but it's also kinda excitin'."

It seems like there're some pervs in your brigade, Captain. At least most of them were just quietly watching.

"Um, Captain? The dish is clean."

The captain chuckled. "Psh. Don't make me laugh. Like hell it's clean after such a short—whoa! It *is*!"

As soon as she rinsed the dish, it had emerged sparklingly white. She was so stunned that her eyes looked like they were about to explode out of her head. *Now, that's what I call a satisfying reaction.*

"Oh, my gosh!" The barmaid washing without soap was also stunned. "I'm nowhere near done over here. Amazing!"

The mercenaries couldn't hide their amazement, either.

"Captain, did you somehow use magic?"

"No, there's no way she did anything like that."

"Then is this the Medicine God's work?!"

Everyone stared at me.

"Ha ha! That's what this liquid does. I promise it's not some special magic," I laughed. "This soap'll make dishwashing a heck of a lot easier, won't it?"

The young barmaid nodded enthusiastically. "Now I won't have to worry about my fingers pruning."

"Even I could do the dishes," the captain said in a low, bemused voice.

I couldn't help but smile. It was almost like watching some punk in my old world do housework successfully for the first time.

"Are you tellin' me you're willin' to do chores, Captain…?" a brigade member asked.

"No! Don't get ahead of yourself," another retorted. "The captain just had to wash dishes to try that strange soap!"

"Amazin'."

"So, these clean dishes are all because of the Medicine God!"

"All right, ladies and gents," I addressed the Red Cat Brigade. "If you could spread your impressions to the rest of the townsfolk, I'd really appreciate it."

"As the Medicine God wishes!"

"As His Divineness wishes!"

"Could you stop calling me that?" I pleaded.

I ended up going to a whole bunch of nearby stores that day to explain how the dish soap worked. I couldn't even begin to describe the shopkeepers' shocked faces and plentiful words of gratitude.

I left the drugstore the next day to make the potion delivery I'd promised, and the Red Cat Brigade's captain was standing right outside.

"Good morning!" I said. "I was just on my way to you guys."

"G-great," she replied. "I, uh, just happened to be passin' by."

She sure is early. Could she really not wait?

I handed the captain the five potions, and she nodded firmly.

"You must really love these potions, Captain," I said. "My little roommate does too. She always begs me for more of them. Just remember, they're medicinal, so don't drink too many."

"Y-yeah, of course," the captain stammered. "Um...I'm Annabelle."

"Oh! I'm Reiji."

"Y-yeah? Well, um, I'll be droppin' by every morning to grab these, so...see ya."

Just like that, Captain Annabelle vanished, almost like she was fleeing a crime scene.

"Hunh. I told her I'd deliver the potions," I mused. "She really didn't have to come out all this way. What a nice gesture."

I'd thought that Annabelle seemed like kind of a brute at first, but clearly, I was wrong. Impressed by her kindness, I headed back inside and opened Kirio Drugs for the day.

10

Kururu's Class Change

I COULD HEAR PEOPLE talking in the storefront. I closed my eyes and focused on the conversation.

"What's up with you?" someone asked.

"U-um, I'm not sure what to say to that," said Mina's voice. "I'm sort of attached to this house, but the other rooms aren't part of the drugstore."

"You mean, you refuse to let me behind the counter?!"

"Er...although you're upset, I..."

From that back-and-forth, it sounded like the customer had some complaints. *They're probably gonna ask for the manager.* In my mind's eye, I could already see a teary-eyed Mina.

I rushed out to the store, calling, "Excuse me, can I help you with something?"

As I expected, Mina's eyes were watering. In front of her was the elf Kururu.

"Mr. Reiji, give me a hand," Mina mumbled.

"Reiji, my dear!" exclaimed Kururu.

Slam! I shut the door to the house tight.

Knock! Knock! Knock! Someone hammered it from the other side.

"Why'd you close the door on me?" called Kururu. "I went out of my way to see you this morning! Just like before...and before that...and before that! Don't be shy!"

"I'm not being *shy*," I replied. "If you don't have actual business here, could you please just go home? You're gonna bother the other customers."

"What're you saying, dear? I specifically visit when there *aren't* other customers! This way, we can be alone together!"

Hunh. He's at least thinking of others, I guess. "It'd be nice if you stopped bothering *me*, too."

Kururu changed the subject. "I noticed a young man visiting your store. Who exactly is he?!"

Was he referring to Zeral? Ever since his fight with Feris, he'd come to the drugstore frequently just to chat. "Hrm. I guess I'd say he's a friend."

"So, you're already intimate?!"

"Jeez. Not that kind of friend. Are you kidding?"

"Fine," said Kururu. "I'll go home for today. See you later, my dear Reiji."

Things went quiet on the other side of the door. I peeked into the drugstore and saw Mina gripping a bouquet.

"Sorry for making you deal with him, Mina," I said. "From now on, if someone annoying pops up, just call me, okay?"

"All right. Thank you very much. Um...he probably intended to give these to you, Mr. Reiji. What should I do with them?"

Oh. Kururu brought that bouquet? Maybe I can use the flowers as ingredients. Otherwise, I don't know. The bouquet did smell good; it was also quite pretty. I was sure Mina would've been delighted to receive something like that under other circumstances.

I glanced at the drugstore entrance absentmindedly, only to see a stunning elf girl cautiously approaching.

"Welcome!" Mina and I said.

"My name's Ririka," the elf girl greeted us. "Um...my big brother's acting weird."

Her "big brother"? Mina tilted her head at me. I responded in kind, communicating via eye contact.

"Um, who's your big brother?" I asked Ririka. "We're not exactly a counseling service—just a pharmacy."

"His name's Kururu, and he's been acting strange recently."

"Recently...?" *You mean, he wasn't an oddball to begin with?*

"Whenever he heads into town, he always seems so restless," Ririka explained. "Today, he took a bouquet, and—well, I followed him. That's when I found this drugstore."

Oh no...this sounds like trouble.

Noticing the bouquet in Mina's hands, Ririka pointed at her. "You're Daisy!"

"'Daisy'?"

Mina and I locked eyes, confused. *Who the heck is Daisy? Beats me.*

Yes, we were in fact conversing via eye contact.

"My brother's always grinning and saying 'Daisy, Daisy' over and over!" Ririka continued. "Don't get all cocky just because you're a little cute!"

Ririka must've been referring to Mina, since the elf girl was pointing at the ghost. She was really angry.

However, Mina didn't seem particularly bothered. She pulled at my sleeve. "Mr. Reiji! Mr. Reiji! She said I'm cute!"

"She did! I'm pretty proud, since you're one of Kirio Drugs' two poster girls."

Thump! Mina hit me lightly.

"Oh, you! Don't expect any special treatment for flattering me...but tonight I'm going to make your favorite for dinner!"

Mina skipped into the back of the house as if flowers were blooming around her.

"Hey! Wait!" Ririka exclaimed.

"You're the one who has to wait," I interjected. "What business do you have with 'Daisy'?"

I'm guessing she misheard "Reiji."

"Er...nothing important," replied Ririka. "I was just upset that my brother's been all weird. I wanted to see who he was meeting, that's all."

Should I really tell her that her brother's into men? It's not my place to come out for him.

"But after seeing you and Daisy talk, I get it," Ririka continued. "She's your girlfriend, isn't she? Yet she's leading my brother on. She'll never get away with this. My poor brother's the victim here!"

Man, Ririka just keeps going on about him. Every time she opens her mouth, it's "brother this" and "brother that." I guess Kururu acts more impressive at home. She must really love the guy.

Now it all made sense. Despite Ririka's prickly attitude, I couldn't help but smile at her. *A worrywart little sister, huh? Heh heh.*

"Wh-what is it? Why're you grinning?"

"No particular reason! Go on. You're jealous that Daisy took your big bro from you, right?"

Poof! Ririka's face turned bright red.

"N-not at all! I just came to see who my belo...er, my brother's so infatuated with! He kept saying Daisy's voice and butt were particularly attractive."

Ugh...

"I-I know it's not my place to butt in," Ririka continued. "B-but it's just...if she's going to become part of our family, I want to know more about her. As Kururu's little sister."

At the end of the day, your big brother's into men. I got that Ririka wanted to watch over Kururu, but this misunderstanding couldn't go on forever. That wouldn't be good for anyone.

With that in mind, I spilled the beans. "I want you to listen very carefully," I told Ririka. "You misheard your brother. He wasn't talking about 'Daisy'; he was talking about 'Reiji.'"

"Huh?" Ririka furrowed her brow.

"And the Reiji he mentioned has a real tough time kicking Kururu out whenever he shows up at the drugstore," I added. "The girl who was here earlier is named Mina. I'm Reiji."

"Wait. That means..."

"Yeah, exactly."

Ririka was unable to hide her shock; her jaw dropped. "Mr. Manager, you like men?"

"How'd you reach that conclusion?! Your *brother* does. I'm into women, but whenever I see Kururu, he goes on and on about me."

"He likes men?! N-no way! My brother's the most popular with the female elves. He's so—"

"I'm telling you the truth."

Ririka looked stunned. "I-I can't believe it." I understood where she was coming from. To her, this must've been a totally new side to her beloved brother.

At any rate, Kururu's actions were becoming a problem for Ririka, too. *Isn't there something I can do about this? I'm guessing Kururu's been so relentless about this because of his over-the-top sex drive.*

"I can't change Kururu, but I might be able to help him reign himself in," I told Ririka.

"Really?!"

"Yeah. First, I'd decrease his sex drive. His personality notwithstanding, his behavior is probably tied to a strong libido."

"Huh? But...um...what would that do to my brother?"

He wouldn't be able to get it up. Which I definitely can't tell Ririka outright.

"He'd chill out for a while." *Okay, that might be too vague.*

"Sounds good," said Ririka. "What should I do after I leave?"

"Hold on a sec. First, I gotta make the prescription."

I grabbed a landen flower off the shelf. The tea I made for Feris had calmed and relaxed her nerves. In other words, it kept her from getting overexcited. *If I strengthen that effect just a little, I should be able to make exactly the medicine I need now.*

As I headed back to the laboratory, Noela saw me and trotted over. "Master, Master! Noela poster girl? Poster girl?"

"Hm? Oh, you mean the thing I told Mina?"

Noela nodded energetically. *She must've overheard when we were talking.*

"Yup. You're my cute little poster girl."

"Arrooo!" Noela wagged her tail, hugging me around the waist.

"Hey, get off! Eh, whatever."

Since Noela refused to leave me alone, I took her with me into the lab and started on the treatment. Eventually, she fell asleep holding her own tail. *She must've gotten bored,* I thought. *Just looking at her heals my tired soul. Hunh...she can stretch her tail out that far?*

I held back the urge to play with Noela and somehow

managed to finish the prescription. I used basically the same process as making herbal tea, just more concentrated. It hadn't taken much time at all.

> **LANDEN EXTRACT (STRONG):** Lowers sex drive by calming nerves.

Hopefully, this landen extract would lessen Kururu's obsession with me. I put a bit into a vial and headed back to the drugstore.

"It doesn't have a strong aroma," I told Ririka, "so you should be able to mix it into food. Just keep in mind that the extract's effect is very strong. You can only use a little at a time."

"All right. Thank you, Reiji!" Ririka grabbed the landen extract from me and rushed out of the drugstore.

Is she gonna be okay? I hope this won't add fuel to the fire.

The next day, my fears turned out to be spot-on. Ririka dashed into the store as soon as I opened up. "Reiji! Sort this out!"

"Er—what?"

Breathless, Ririka pointed behind her. I cautiously craned my neck and saw Kururu approaching us.

"Ah, good morning," I greeted him. "You two are together today, huh?"

"Sure are," Kururu replied. "Gosh, this goody-two-shoes! I swear, as soon as we woke up this morning, she just babbled on and on about how I was acting—like, come on, Ririka! Then she dragged me all the way here. Can you just, like, believe her?"

Hunh. His voice is still deep, but he almost sounds like an okama.

"Need an explanation?" Ririka cried.

Nope.

She clutched my shoulders and shook me. "What am I going to do, Reiji?! My brother—he's unrecognizable!"

"How much landen extract did you put into his food?"

"I wanted him to control his libido, so I put it all in his dinner last night!"

"There's your problem. Didn't I tell you only to use a little?"

"Oh my gosh, Ririka," Kururu interrupted. "Why are you acting, like, all clingy with Reiji? When we get home, I'm gonna totes tell you off." He glanced at me. "Like, women, am I right?"

For some reason, Kururu now had an *okama*-style cleft chin. Seriously.

I rubbed my eyes and took another look. *Yup. Cleft chin, right there. Weird. That wasn't listed as one of the landen extract's effects.*

I told Ririka to take a deep breath. "The extract's effects aren't permanent. He should go back to normal eventually. His chin, too."

Ririka looked relieved. "Th-thank goodness. No more side effects."

Sadly, my landen extract hadn't had any effect on Kururu's overconfidence.

"His face is strangely pudgy, too," Ririka added. "Will that go back to normal? Along with his chin?"

"Whoa—you're right, it is. Don't worry, that should go away with his chin cleft."

Three days later, the usual Kururu strolled into the drugstore with a refreshed smile, his chin cleft gone.

With this trial run in mind, I decided not to sell the landen extract. Somehow, however, word got out about the treatment, and wives with cheating husbands visited in droves.

I made a point of warning each and every one of them about the extract's effects. "Just be careful. If you use it wrong, your husband might end up with some pretty unexpected side effects."

11

A Struggle Against Aging

SALES ROSE, and the amount of time I dedicated to making medicine went up. The drugstore's selection grew quite nicely. As a result, I had lots of free time behind the counter at the drugstore, chilling and staring off into space.

"You're zoning out again, Manager," Mikoto said as I daydreamed.

She was here from the next village over to buy medicine. She was probably fifteen or sixteen—a cheerful, ordinary girl with wavy black hair.

"That's Mr. Manager to you," I replied.

"Three potions and three energy drinks!"

"Haven't you ever heard of saying please?"

"Don't sweat it! Me and you are already besties."

"Since when?" I grabbed the potions off the shelf and bagged them.

Mikoto handed me the money. We shot the breeze for a bit, and then she pointed at the door and informed me of a customer. An old butler, apparently.

"Welcome," I said.

"Are you Sir Reiji?" asked the elderly man.

"Yes, that'd be me."

"My name's Rayne. I serve Lord Casty Fen Dran Valgas. I'm here to summon you to the mansion on behalf of Lord Valgas's wife, Lady Flam."

"Er—um—who?"

"Count Casty Fen Dran Valgas is the lord who governs our villages, Manager," Mikoto explained.

Lord Valgas is a nobleman? Why would nobility—the count's wife, at that—summon me, of all people?

"As for this invitation's purpose, Lady Flam said she wishes to explain it in person," Rayne continued. "I'd like you to accompany me to the mansion immediately."

What is this, a kidnapping? Meh. It's not like I'm busy.

"Sure, fine," I replied. "Mikoto, watch over the store for me."

"Since when are you my boss?!"

"You don't have anything better to do, do you? If you have any problems, just grab Mina."

I waved to her and got into the carriage parked outside with Rayne the butler.

It took the shaky carriage about fifteen minutes to arrive at the manor. Rayne led me inside, guiding me through a lavishly decorated hall.

He knocked on an equally lavish door. "Sir Reiji has arrived, Milady."

"You may enter."

Rayne opened the door for me, and I headed inside.

"So, you're the genius alchemist everyone's been talking about," Lady Flam greeted me. "Have a seat."

I sat down as instructed. "Um, 'genius alchemist' isn't quite right. But, yes, that's me."

Lady Flam wore a luxurious outfit suitable for a noble-woman; she waved an expensive-looking hand fan. In terms of her demeanor, she certainly seemed like a snooty old lady. Honestly, she was exactly what I'd imagined a rich person in this world would be like.

"What business do you have with me?" I asked. "Rayne told me that you wished to speak directly."

"Allow me to get to the point," said Lady Flam. "I'd like you to make a de-aging medication."

De-aging medication? I could imagine the ingredients, but I doubted I could get my hands on them anytime soon. *Still, the fact that I can actually make one at all is kind of nuts.* "What's the deadline?"

"Five days from now. Wait, no. The dinner party's in five days, so could you bring me the treatment by that afternoon?"

Okay. Now I see the full picture. She wants the other nobles at this party to go crazy over how young she looks.

"That's not enough time. I won't be able to make the treatment on that schedule," I stated firmly.

She slouched in disappointment. "Then I suppose I must resign myself to the prince gossiping about how I've aged."

"Aged?! That's not true at all! Lady Flam, you're as beautiful and young as anyone!" I exclaimed. If I'd learned one irrefutable rule in any society, it was that complimenting women was always a good idea.

Lady Flam slapped open her fan and covered her mouth with it. "I-Is that so?" she asked, trying to hide her happiness. "It's no good. Even if you feel that way, the prince surely won't."

I honestly felt bad for her. Tearing her down because of her looks was just plain old bullying. There was nothing she could do about getting older.

I wanted to help Lady Flam. Still, I couldn't make a de-aging potion in only five days. "Wait, so I just need to do something about your wrinkles?"

"*Excuse* me?"

Whoops. She sure didn't let that one slip by. "Sorry! No offense meant. Ha ha...!"

"Sir Alchemist, can you do something to help me? I have plenty of money."

"If I create a treatment, I'll be more than happy to accept the appropriate payment."

If I did something about her wrinkled skin, she'd certainly look younger. At least, that was the basic idea I'd come up with. I probably wasn't too far from the right answer; even I, as a guy, saw that Lady Flam's skin was aging. If someone like me could tell at first glance, her peers most certainly could.

"All right, I see," I said. "I'll do what I can. I may not be able to literally de-age you, but I'll try to mix something to make you *look* younger."

"Oh, my! Really?" exclaimed Lady Flam. "I'll finally defeat the curse of aging?"

"I wouldn't go that far, but..."

"Sir Genius Alchemist, you truly defy even God's will!"

"Yeah, okay, enough of that."

Apparently deeply moved by my determination to

help her, Lady Flam then listed off the top ten awful insults other aristocrats had lobbed at her.

This isn't doing much for my motivation, I'm not gonna lie. It seemed like I'd be stuck listening to her complaints all day. "Okay, I'm gonna get to work, so I need to head back to my drugstore."

I fled from the mansion in Lady Flam's horse and carriage as quickly as possible.

Back at Kirio Drugs, I grabbed some ingredients—goat's milk, a pear-like fruit, and various medicinal petals—from the kitchen. Holed up in the laboratory, I combined all the ingredients.

> **BEAUTY GEL:** Moisturizer. Makes skin fairer and more supple. Prevents dry skin.

"It's done!" The beauty gel was more of a cream than a liquid.

I got directions to the lord's mansion from Mina, then followed the route with the finished product in hand. Finally, I arrived at the huge estate. The elderly butler, Rayne, came out to meet me after I stated my business, and once again led me to Lady Flam's room.

"What's the matter, Sir Alchemist?" Lady Flam inquired. "Is there something you'd like to ask?"

"No. I just wrapped up, so I'm here to deliver the finished product."

"Pardon me—did you say 'finished product'?" Lady Flam seemed utterly confused.

I whipped out the freshly made beauty gel and passed it to her. "Massage this beauty gel on your face just after getting out of the bath. Make sure you do it every day."

"Y-you want me to put this on my face every day?!" Lady Flam cast me a doubtful look. "Sir Alchemist, I trust you aren't trying to play me for a fool."

"Even if I am, what's the worst that could happen? How about giving it a try? If you get no results, you don't have to pay me."

"Hrm." She opened the bottle and sniffed; her eyebrows rose in surprise. "What a delightful aroma."

"Well, the gel contains flowers and fruit."

"It's just... Massage it on my face...?"

I spread some gel on the back of her hand. Fortunately, it blended just fine with her skin. Still, Lady Flam seemed hesitant.

"I'm not the one who's going to be humiliated at that dinner party," I pointed out. "That's *you*, right? If you refuse to use this, then it's all over."

"Hrm...if you truly believe this cream will work, I suppose I can at least try it. I'm quite tired of being a laughingstock."

"Then let's make them all swallow their words!"

At my call to arms, Lady Flam nodded intently, and so her week-long battle against her age began. That said, I didn't actually witness it in person. Rayne would drop in at the drugstore to update me. Lady Flam apparently made sure to apply the cream every night, as directed.

On the fifth day, I found it odd that Rayne hadn't yet dropped in. Just as I began to ponder what had happened, I noticed a horse and carriage parking outside the store. Lo and behold, Lady Flam had come.

Er...seriously? This isn't exactly what I expected. Her face...even her skin... She was matronly before. Now, she looks more like a young woman. She seems happy as can be, too.

"How do I look, Sir Alchemist?"

"Wonderful! You really gave it a shot, huh?"

"I don't know how I can ever thank you," she added as Rayne took out a wallet.

"Now, now. Let's not talk about that yet. You're about to head to the dinner party, right? I'm more than happy to accept payment after you show those fools what's what."

Lady Flam instructed Rayne to put the wallet away. The pair got back into her carriage, heading to wherever the party was being held.

I'm sure my new beauty gel had an effect, but I'd also say that she gained a bit of self-confidence. If so, this was all worth it.

A few days later, I received payment for the de-aging treatment—and tons of boxes of apparently pricey sweets. There was even a thank you card. Inside, Lady Flam expressed her triumphant feelings about the whole situation, and she couldn't stop thanking me.

The mountain of sweets amazed Mina and Noela.

"Aaah!" Mina gasped. "Mr. Reiji! Mr. Reiji! These are super-expensive, super-sweet delicacies! Where'd you get them?!"

"I helped a noblewoman out. This was her way of expressing her gratitude."

Noela, of course, had already ripped into one box. She sank to the floor and dug into the sweets like a machine.

"Tasty, tasty!" Her tail slapped the floor lightly. She looked as though she was about to melt from glee on the spot.

Seeing Noela so satisfied, I decided to grab one myself. *From a modern-day Japanese perspective, I'd say this is maybe a tad too sugary. Still plenty tasty, though!*

"If you eat too many, you're not going to have room for dinner, Noela," said Mina, munching the desserts just as quickly.

"Mina, I know they're good and all, but you're gonna put on weight," I remarked.

"Nngh! Wh-why would you go and say something like that? Mr. Reiji, you big meanie! Now I can't even enjoy these in peace!" Mina cried, her mouth still full. Clearly, my comment was nothing against her sweet tooth.

Either way, Lady Flam was ecstatic, and Noela and Mina were thrilled with the abundant sweets. Being surrounded by those happy women, well, that made for one extremely happy day.

12

Be Careful How You Use It

*D*ING, DONG! *Ding, dong!*

I opened the store to the sound of a bell ringing in the distance, and saw that Kalta was oddly busy. *What's going on?*

It wasn't long before Annabelle of the Red Cat Brigade, the town's security force, dropped in. She normally had the eyes of a bird of prey—kind of scary, actually—but that look was nowhere to be found today.

She shot me the same piercing gaze as always, but there was no strength behind it. "G'morning."

"Good morning! It looks busy out there. What's going on?" I asked, trying to sound casual, while I prepared her usual five potions.

"Sorry, but could I get ten today?" Annabelle inquired.

"Sure, but you'll have to pay extra."

"Oh, yeah. Of course."

Taking the money from her, I added another five potion bottles. "You sure do love these, huh?"

"I haven't been the one drinking them recently," she said, turning to leave the drugstore. "Well, anyway, thanks as always."

But before she could go through the door, Doz, a knucklehead from the Red Cat Brigade, ran in. "Ah, Boss!"

"Why're you here, Doz?" Annabelle barked.

Doz looked down guiltily. "You said you were heading back to the barracks."

"I hope you didn't come in to tell Reiji anything *weird*."

"But, Boss—"

"But goddamn *nothing*! Why the hell does a pharmacist have to hear our dirty laundry? Do you really wanna embarrass the Red Cat Brigade this bad?!"

"No, not at all! But at this rate..."

"What's going on, guys?" I interrupted. "If I can, I'd love to help."

"Thanks so much, bro," Doz replied. "Did you hear about the bandits who've been coming to town recently?"

Annabelle ran her hands through her red hair. "Fine, fine. I'll explain, Doz. Back down."

Doz nodded and fell in behind her. This didn't seem like a conversation to have standing around in the drugstore, so I invited them into the house, putting a little sign that read "In the back" on the counter.

Since I didn't have a reception area or anything, I took them into the living room and let them sit on the sofa. "So, what's going on? It seems pretty serious."

"Yeah, well, like Doz said, some bastards have been coming to Kalta to steal stuff," explained Annabelle. "There've already been a whole bunch of victims. And the lord hired the Red Cat Brigade to keep the peace, right? Well, he's threatening not to pay us if things keep going this way."

Doz nodded sadly. "We're doing our best, bro. But these bandits are tough cookies. Just this morning, our men fought 'em while patrolling."

So, that's what all that noise was. Wait. Did Annabelle buy extra potions because brigade members got injured? She did say she wasn't the one drinking them recently. If bandits ever attacked me, I'd give them my cash immediately—I'm no veteran mercenary. This is some scary stuff. It sounds like the only reason I've been able to live here in peace is because the Red Cat Brigade protects Kalta's residents under the radar.

"If the lord stops paying us, we'll have to quit and look for other gigs," Doz added. "Us mercs gotta eat to live, you know? I was hoping we could maybe borrow some of that wisdom of yours, Reiji, bro."

"Which is why you ran into me, eh?" Annabelle asked Doz.

I guessed that she didn't want Doz bringing this issue to me because guarding Kalta was their job. Mercenaries were professional fighters, so what did seeking help from a complete amateur say about them? Annabelle's pride wouldn't allow Doz to do something like that.

"Is the Red Cat Brigade the town's only security?"

"The lord has his personal guard, but his best fighters are on the front lines, battling the Demon King's armies," Annabelle replied. "The only knights left here are older."

"Reiji, bro, I don't want you to think we can't do our jobs. We're always repelling and capturing bandits," Doz said.

"You mentioned that these guys are particularly strong. Are they a different group than usual?"

"Yeah. We got no clue where they came from, but they're definitely experienced."

That made the Red Cat Brigade want my assistance. Sadly, I was neither a genius nor a warrior. All I could really do was make medicine. *Hrm.*

"I just thought maybe you'd be able to help us," Doz added.

"I hate needin' backup on crap like this! That's why

I told you to cut it out, Doz," Annabelle interjected. "Reiji's someone we should protect, not get help from!"

"Don't worry about that, Annabelle," I reassured her. "The Red Cat Brigade is the only reason people like me can live comfortably in Kalta. Please, let me stick my nose in your business— just as a one-off."

"The Medicine God's descended!" Doz exclaimed.

I couldn't help but chuckle. "Are these bandits so strong that you guys are no match?"

"No, it's not that bad. If we give 'em an opening, though, they're quick to take it." Annabelle's tone clearly signaled that she was disappointed in herself and her men.

Kalta wasn't protected by brick walls or a moat or anything like that—there was just a log fence marking the edges of town. Strengthening that light defense would take too much time and effort.

"The answer ain't to improve our equipment," Annabelle continued, "but to focus on fightin' the bandits back directly."

While I was thinking, Noela's voice rang out from the kitchen. "Mina! Tears won't stop! Keep coming!"

"Are you all right, Noela?" Mina replied. "You have to be careful when you peel onions."

"Aroo...!" Noela sniffled.

Are they getting lunch ready? They honestly sounded

like sisters, which was more than enough to put a smile on my face. *Oh, wait! I could make* that.

I turned to Doz. "I need you to buy me booze with the highest alcohol content you can find."

"Sure. You plannin' on a bender?"

"I'll be using it in medicine. I'm counting on you."

Doz stood and headed out, a bit confused.

"If there's anything I can do, I'll do it," Annabelle said.

"Thanks a ton. Come with me." We rose and made our way to the kitchen.

"Ah!" exclaimed Mina. "We're making lunch, Mr. Reiji."

"Awesome."

"Noela helping too, Master!"

I patted the puffy-eyed Noela on the head. She closed her eyes. *I guess that tickles a little.*

"Heartwarmin'," Annabelle whispered to herself, somewhat shocked. Mina smiled welcomingly at her.

"I'm looking forward to lunch," I said. "By the way, Mina, do you have any of *those*? You know."

"Erm...I'm not sure I do."

"You know—those spicy things you bought before."

"Oh, these!" Mina pulled three green vegetables from a box.

"Yeah, that's it! Thanks! Could I use them? I'll make sure to buy you extras at the market later."

"You're going to make medicine from spicy capshins?"

I nodded and entered the lab. Since Annabelle didn't really have any way to help, she simply observed my process, letting out a few interested, surprised noises as she watched. "So, that's how you've been makin' medicine. Wow."

It would've been awkward if she hadn't reacted at all, but it was also kind of hard to work with her watching so intently.

Doz soon returned, out of breath, with the alcohol I requested. "Boss, Reiji, this is the strongest booze they got. Drink some on a cold day, and you'll be fast asleep!"

"Don't talk it up. I'm not gonna drink any of it."

Looking kind of disappointed, Doz watched me work with Annabelle. "So, this is how he makes our potions."

"That's what I just said."

"Hunh. Imagine that!"

These two are pretty tight, huh? I shook the finished product, and it glowed as usual.

CAPSHIN FLUID (STRONG): Irritant. Harmless to the human body. Vaporizes upon contact with air. Immediately causes severe eye pain, breathlessness, and mucus production.

"All right. Perfect." I loosened my grip on the terrifying mixture. *I need to move this to a smaller bottle.*

"Reiji, bro—no, Medicine God—did you make us somethin'?"

"Yup. When you get close to this liquid..." I opened the bottle slowly.

"The liquid in that bottle?" Doz drew close. It turned out to be perfect timing. "Gaaaaaaah! My eyes! Aaah! Ow ow ow...!"

He covered his face with both hands and writhed on the floor, coughing. Tears and snot ran down his face.

Super effective.

"Ah ha ha ha ha! You big dummy!" Annabelle laughed as she looked down at her panicking subordinate. "Whew! Man, what the heck's up with this weird liquid? All you did was mix spicy capshins with booze!"

"Er, you shouldn't get too close," I warned her.

"Ain't you a man of the Red Cat Brigade?" she asked Doz, leaning toward the capshin fluid. "How sa—aaaaahhh! What's *happening*?! My eyes, my eyes! Auuugh—they sting! Gaaaaah!"

Coughing in pain, Annabelle joined Doz on the floor.

I let out a resigned sigh. *It's like tear gas you can throw at the enemy to push them back,* I mused, pouring some capshin fluid into a vial. "What were you thinking,

Annabelle? Did you not just see what happened to Doz? Aren't you supposed to be the Red Cat Brigade's—"

Just then, my hand slipped, and the larger bottle shattered on the floor.

"Ah."

The capshin fluid's effects overwhelmed me immediately. "Gaaaaaaah! My eyes, my eyes! Ow, ow, ow, ow, ow! It hurts! What the hell?! No, no, no, no! This is freaking awful! I'm gonna die! My eyes!"

I collapsed, wheezing, my hands over my face. I just barely heard Noela in the room's entrance. "Mina? Master on floor. Everyone on floor."

"Mr. Reiji's in the middle of work, Noela. Come now, let's prepare lunch."

"Grrr."

No, no! Mina, Noela! This isn't work! But no matter what, I couldn't react.

It took about twenty minutes for Annabelle, Doz, and I to recover from the capshin fluid. I made sure to explain that it shouldn't cause lasting effects.

"I understand," Doz said. "Bro, you made somethin' crazy."

"Y-yeah," Annabelle agreed.

"But with this stuff, we'll be able to chase those bandits off, no sweat! We can even capture them!"

I tried to hand Annabelle six bottles of the capshin fluid, but she motioned to Doz. "You take these."

"Huh? B-Boss, I don't wanna."

"W-well, I'm the brigade captain. So, uh, it ain't my job to carry 'em." Her voice was very faint.

"Um...Reiji, bro? Could you deliver these to the barracks for us?"

"Wha...? Uh...well...um...I still, uh, have work to do. And I'm, uh, busy. Yeah. Sorry."

In the end, Doz wound up carrying the bottles back. The capshin liquid was so strong, it'd traumatized all three of us. However, I kept one bottle for myself. Self-defense purposes.

◆◆◆

Late that evening, I awoke to the sound of the village bell ringing. *Ding, dong! Ding, dong!*

Worried that there might be a fire or something, I headed outside immediately. Then I noticed three Red Cat Brigade members outside Kalta's gate, squaring off with six bandits.

The mercenaries held the bottles I'd given Doz and Annabelle. They threw them at the bandits, and the bottles shattered. *Smash! Smash!*

"Gaaaaaaaaaaaah!" The bandits dropped their swords and spears, writhing on the ground in pain.

Yeah, I've been there, guys. I knew I shouldn't sympathize, considering that they were criminals and all. After experiencing the pain firsthand, however, I couldn't help it. *Man, that sucked.*

In the end, there was no grand standoff, no epic fight to defend Kalta. Nothing. It all ended with the mercenaries catching the six bandits. The next day, Annabelle popped up at the drugstore to thank me and explain that the town was at peace again.

I was proud that I'd made such a strong defensive weapon, but I had no intention of mass-producing capshin fluid. If it were on the open market, people could use it for all sorts of bad things. I had to make sure I only mixed it on request.

I gotta be careful with this power of mine.

13

The Drills Cometh

"**M**ASTER. Drills. Drills here."

I was holed up in my laboratory when Noela came in talking about drills. *What the heck?* She was supposed to be watching the storefront, so I guessed she must've been referring to a customer.

"Ask for you, Master. Drills."

"Er...me?" *Wonder what they want. And what does Noela mean, "drills"?*

I headed for the storefront and noticed a girl at the counter. *Ah. That's what she meant.*

Noela was right on the money. The girl wore a knee-length gothic dress and had long ringlets, their shape similar to the spiral drills I'd seen carpenters use. Judging by the way she held herself, she'd had a high-class upbringing. That said, she seemed a little bit uneasy.

At first glance, she looked about the age of a junior high student.

"Welcome! What can I help you with?" I asked.

"Are you this pharmacy's owner?"

Her tone struck me as fairly snobbish. *I feel like I met someone recently with a similar attitude.* "Yeah. I'm Kirio Reiji."

"My name's Elaine Fen Dran Valgas."

"Hunh. Is that so?"

Elaine smacked the counter, clearly displeased with my nonchalance. "Don't 'is that so' me! Show some respect!"

"Look, young lady. If you want people around you to show respect, you need to show them respect first." I wasn't exactly perfect in that regard, but I was certainly more polite than some kid. "That's the first rule of being a grown-up. Got it?"

"D-don't treat me like a child!"

But you are one.

"I'm a gentlewoman. The day after tomorrow, my father and I will attend a formal dinner party. I am a genuine *lady*!"

"Hunh."

Elaine struck the counter again. "Do not 'hunh' me! You're supposed to be *surprised*!"

"So, you're here to buy something, then? Do you have enough allowance? I don't sell candy."

"Hmph. Fine. I'm not here to buy anything."

"Then why'd you come in?"

Elaine cleared her throat. "I heard about you from my mother."

"And who would that be?"

"Her name is Flam."

"Ah, Lady Flam. So, you're her daughter."

"Precisely." Elaine placed both hands on her hips triumphantly.

That does make her a noble. I suppose that explains why she's being so bratty and pretentious.

"I heard all about you from Mother," Elaine continued. "You're a genius who rebels against the gods themselves."

"What the heck did Flam fill your head with? Seriously." Elaine had literally gotten everything wrong so far.

"You de-aged her with a potion you mixed, didn't you? If you can perform such miracles, perhaps you can create the item I desire."

"Well, it depends what exactly that is, and how much time it'd take."

"I'd like to request popularity po—"

"Like hell!" *Popularity potion?! I mean, I'd make that for* myself *first!*

"But why not?" Elaine pouted. "You were willing to accept Mother's request, but not mine?! It isn't very professional for a shopkeeper to change their attitude based on the customer."

I could envision a "popularity" treatment with my medicine-making skill, so it was definitely possible. But the ingredients would be a hassle to get. "When exactly would you need this?"

"The day after next!"

"Sorry, but it's a no-go. I told your mother—I can't just make stuff on the fly without any prep time."

"But...you still mixed her de-aging potion, did you not?"

"Here's the thing, young lady. I actually made a separate treatment *similar* to what she wanted, not a de-aging potion."

Elaine went quiet. She must've thought I was a guaranteed solution to her woes.

"Need anything else? If not, I'll have Noela come back to watch the store."

"Noela?"

"The beastling—er, I mean, werewolf girl—out here earlier."

Noela got angry when I called her a beastling. "Master wrong! Noela no beastling! Werewolf!" she'd say, pouting in my direction. The problem was, she was so cute when she did that, I couldn't help teasing her. Truth be told, she was the only one of her kind I'd ever met, so I had no clue what the difference was between beastlings and werewolves.

"Don't get her yet," said Elaine. "I want to know why you can't create a popularity treatment for me. Aren't you a genius alchemist?"

"No, actually, I'm a pharmacist. Got it? Someone who makes medicine."

"Hmm? Yes, an alchemist. Mother told me that medicine making is basically alchemy."

"Your mom needs a lesson on the word 'basically'! Look, even without a popularity potion, you're already a cute young lady."

Elaine didn't even pretend to react to the praise. "Well, of course."

As nobility, she must be used to that sort of praise. "This is the part when you deny it."

"But, as I said, all manner of aristocrats will attend the dinner," Elaine continued.

"Mm-hmm."

"I'll be greeting other families, dancing, and dining. There will be all sorts of delicious food that would astonish a commoner like you."

Honestly, I'd prefer Mina's food anyway. "Yes, yes. And?"

"Lord Lars of the Gallardo family will be there, and... um..." Elaine fidgeted as her cheeks turned red.

Hrm. So, she likes this Lars fellow. "And that's why you want a popularity potion?"

"Yes. U-um, wait—no! It's just that Lord Lars is a count's second son. His family's on equal footing with mine, and, um... Well, as far as I'm concerned, I could certainly do better, but—"

"Yeah, yeah. I get it, young lady. You're the most gorgeous girl ever."

"Are you making fun of me?"

"Yup. Glad you noticed."

"You're supposed to deny it! You *are* making fun of me!"

I couldn't help letting out a belly laugh. "Think about it this way," I suggested. "If you don't use a popularity potion, this Lars guy might never fall for you. But if you didn't *keep* using the potion, he wouldn't *stay* in love with you. Wouldn't that be kind of sad?"

"Grrr! For a commoner, you have a lot of nerve!"

"Before resorting to a potion, how about trying to win his heart on your own? Being popular isn't easy, and it isn't necessarily connected to love, right?"

"How dare you speak as though you know me, commoner?!"

"Commoner, noble—none of that has anything to do with this."

"Grr! I hate that I don't know what to say to that."

"Hrmph."

Hey, it's me—the adult man proudly debating a school-girl. I can talk all I want, but the truth is, I have no clue about any of this. I've never tried to be popular.

"What should I do to catch Lord Lars's eye, then?"

It was my turn to fall silent, but I soon realized that I had to say something.

I squeezed some words out painfully. "Well, um, let's see. Look... No, the popularity potion isn't gonna happen, but I might be able to make a treatment that'll help."

Elaine leaned over the counter excitedly. "You can?! Really?!"

"There's no guarantee, but...I think I could make a potion that draws out your charm."

"I have money! As much as you desire! Once I head back to the mansion—"

"You dummy." I smacked her head lightly.

"Eeek! H-how dare you hit me!"

"Don't patronize adults, Drills. Hold on a sec."

Leaving Elaine in the drugstore, I headed to my laboratory to start on my prototype. "God. That's why dealing with rich people is such a pain. Everything's money, money, money. I'm not taking money from a dang kid."

Mina peeked in. "Um, Mr. Reiji? Should I serve her tea?"

"We ain't got tea for that stupid set of drills." *Stupid* because *of her drill hair? Or does she have drills because she's stupid? Jury's out.*

"Hee hee!" Mina giggled. "She looked as if she had such fun talking to you. Noela's keeping her company right now."

Hm? Noela?

I heard Elaine's voice. "So, you're Noela? You're the first beastling I've ever met. I'd love it if we could be—"

She'd immediately stepped on a landmine. "Noela no beastling!"

Noela stomped back into the lab, pouting angrily. "Master! Noela hate Drills!"

I grabbed her cheeks in both hands and squished them all over.

"What about me, Noela?" Mina asked.

"Love Mina."

"Yay!" Mina hugged Noela tightly.

As this warm sight unfolded beside me, I got back to work. As usual, I bottled the finished treatment and shook it, making it glow.

> **CHARM FRAGRANCE:** A unique perfume with a fresh fruit scent.

"Perfect." I didn't know whether Elaine would like it, but...

Mina and Noela looked over. "What's up?" I asked.

"Smell nice!"

"If you put some on, you'll smell good, too."

"I'd like to try some, Mr. Reiji," Mina requested.

"Sure."

"Oh! But are you certain someone like myself can..."

"Fine, then. No."

"Gosh! Don't be such a meanie!"

"Heh heh. Later, okay? This is specifically for Elaine," I informed Mina, heading back to the drugstore counter.

"The popularity potion's d-done?!" The young girl rushed up to me.

I took a moment to calm her down. "Just to be clear, this *isn't* a popularity potion. It's something called 'perfume,' and it smells great. I'm gonna show you how to use it, so make sure you follow my instructions. If you can, you'll be twice as ladylike."

Elaine's thin throat gulped loudly. "T-twice as ladylike...? That would make me incredibly popular!"

"This is just a scent, okay? Your attitude, the way you hold yourself—any of that could render this moot."

She swallowed again. "I-I understand."

She was cute when she wasn't being conceited. I dripped a couple droplets of the bottled liquid onto Elaine's wrist, then had her rub it gently against her other wrist.

"Ah! It smells delightful. But when I rub my wrists against each other, the scent isn't as pronounced. Are you sure this is right?"

"If you put too much on, it ends up having the opposite effect."

"Really? You're sure knowledgeable about all sorts of things."

"No—it's just that you're not."

"Grr...couldn't you have phrased that more gently? I'll have you know I am, in fact, the ruling lord's daughter."

"Oh. I almost forgot," I chuckled. "Next is your neck."

"I suppose that nothing I say about my status gets through to you. What a strange man you are," Elaine said, giggling quietly. "There doesn't appear to be much of this scent. I'll make sure only to use a little when I absolutely have to."

"Exactly. That's the right approach."

After I gave Elaine a short lecture on using perfume, Rayne—the elderly butler from before—came into the drugstore, panting.

"M-Milady, I've been looking for you!" Apparently, Elaine came here without permission.

"Oh, my. It appears I've been discovered. Thank you very much for the medicine, Sir Reiji. Have a wonderful day!" She bowed her head and curtsied elegantly.

"Go kick some butt at that dinner party. Got it?"

Elaine's face suddenly turned bright red. "Wh-what're you implying, all of a sudden? You don't have to tell me that! Besides, I'm an attractive noblewoman. Th-there's nothing to be concerned about."

The young lady turned away and finally headed home with her butler.

She's at that age when kids are more in love with the idea of love. It's not particularly uncommon for things to go badly. At any rate, I hope the perfume helps her out.

◆◉◆

A couple days later, Elaine returned to the drugstore alone.

"What's up?" I asked. "Isn't the dinner party today?"

"Oh, well...I decided not to go." Her voice had gotten quiet.

"Did something happen?"

"A-after some thought, I had the feeling that, um, a gentleman who addressed me frankly and honestly would suit me b-better. I-I, um, care little about house or class." She appeared to shrink as she continued her explanation. "I'm more attracted to people with talent."

"Hunh. Really?"

"Many nobles act high and mighty and care only for status."

"Pot. Kettle. Black." *She's totally pretending she didn't do that just a few days ago.*

"I realized I have no interest in people like that," Elaine continued. "And, when I thought more about it, I noticed Lord Lars wasn't actually my type."

"Hunh. Well, that's fine, I suppose. So, what brings you here today?"

"Nothing in particular. It's just...I wondered whether I could help you somehow."

"Help me? Hrm. Wait a sec...are you wearing the charm perfume?"

Fwoop! Elaine hopped away. "Y-yes, um, I put some on! I hope it's not unpleasant."

"No, not at all. It smells great. It's just—why today?"

Glancing into the house, I noticed Noela cross her arms. "Drills no good, Master."

What's going on?

Elaine stuck around for a bit, chatting away, before Rayne eventually arrived to fetch her. Once she was gone, Noela entered the drugstore. She waved her arms, attempting to get rid of the perfume scent.

Why is she doing that?

Off to the side, Mina giggled. "It appears that Noela has a rival."

"Wha...?"

Noela huffed and puffed. "Drills no good, Master."

"Er...yeah, sure," I replied halfheartedly.

She nodded, satisfied.

14

Friendship is Priceless

"**W**HAT DO YOU THINK, Noela?"

"No good."

"Yeah."

The two of us were in our usual forest. This had been a great spot because the more dangerous monsters and beasts didn't come anywhere near. Lately, however, we must've harvested a bit too much—there weren't nearly as many medicinal plants as usual. I had some stocked in the laboratory, so it wasn't an immediately pressing issue, but still.

I let out a small sigh. "What do you think we should do, Noela?"

She answered so fast that it was actually sort of startling. "No clue."

Well, if numbers are down, we just gotta get them back up. So, how do I help grow plants around here? I bet alchemy would be real useful for something like that.

Frustrated, I looked at the ground, noticing something that resembled sesame seeds around my toes.

> **TORIGISOU SEEDS:** Blossom into yellow flowers. Leaves/ stems are medicinal.

I took a quick look around, spotting the same seeds elsewhere. *Hrm. Guess it's time to plant some of these seeds, then.*

"Noela? Can you gather any seeds that look like these?"

"Seeds? All right. Noela gather."

We spent about an hour searching for torigisou seeds before heading back home.

I'd put Mina on shop duty while we were gone. She tilted her head at us, puzzled, as we came in. "Oh, you didn't gather any plants today? Did something happen?"

"Yup. We've foraged a little too much in the forest recently; there weren't many herbs growing. We're thinking of planting more ourselves. Look—seeds."

"Oh, I see," replied Mina. "Gracious, Mr. Reiji. That's a really good idea. So many people just take and take without ever thinking about what they're doing. But you're going to grow herbs yourself!"

"Please, I'm not doing anything special. Growing these will help the drugstore, too."

"Still, I think it's wonderful that you're letting the forest herbs grow back."

"Master wonderful! Thoughtful." Noela stood up straight and patted my head. It was actually kind of embarrassing, since I was usually the one dishing out pats.

"Will you grow them in pots?" Mina asked. "If so, you might have too many seeds."

"I was just thinking about that. If we pot them, we won't grow enough for the drugstore. I figured maybe I could rent land from someone."

"I see," she replied. "In that case, I believe a man named Mr. Alonzo has a large field. You might want to talk to him."

Like Noela, Mina was one of my counter girls. The adorable beastling and cute, soothing ghost were a killer pair, if I did say so myself. I knew full well that the neighborhood housewives chatted with Mina when she worked in the drugstore, which was why she was so knowledgeable about Kalta.

"Reiji! Reiji, I need your help!"

That voice... I turned, somewhat annoyed, to find Zeral standing there. Zeral *Alonzo.* The Alonzo whom Mina mentioned was, in fact, him.

Since Kirio Drugs had solved Zeral's little problem, he returned every time something happened between him and his girlfriend.

"Don't tell me you got into another fight with Feris? This isn't an emergency shelter."

"Come on, don't be like that."

"Though I do have something to discuss with you." I explained the herb situation to Zeral, and he immediately gave me permission to grow them.

"Of course! I owe you!"

"Are you sure? Don't you need to ask your family?"

"Ah ha ha ha! It's fine. Don't worry about it. I'm the Alonzo family's head."

Apparently, his family were landlords, and quite wealthy. That was why Zeral got to spend his days flirting with his girlfriend.

Argh. He has a girlfriend, and he doesn't even have to work? He's got it made. Man, reality kinda blows, even in another world.

"Huh? Are you all right, Reiji? You seem kinda down in the dumps."

"It's nothing."

"Anyway, yeah, I can lend you a field or two."

"That'll be pricey, though, right?" I asked. "Landlords

usually profit off farmers. You know, sucking up taxes and stuff."

"Ah ha ha ha!" Zeral laughed loudly. "Yeah, there're definitely folks like that out there, but I'd never do something so awful. I'm not gonna take any money from you. Use the fields however you'd like."

"Despite all the relationship troubles, you're a good dude."

"Come now, we're friends. Of course I'll give you a hand."

Friends, huh? I think this is the first time anyone's ever said that to me outright—it isn't something people usually put into words, in my experience at least. Hearing Zeral say it gave me pause, but honestly, it also made me happy.

Clap, clap, clap! Beside us, Mina applauded. "Wonderful! I'm so glad you've made a friend, Mr. Reiji. You're always out in the woods, or holed up making medicine. I was worried!"

"Noela relieved!"

"We're going to celebrate!" Mina continued. "You'll have something delicious waiting when you finish work!"

"Oh man, we can't celebrate *that*. It's way too embarrassing! Please, I'm begging you!"

"Aw. Are you sure?" Mina looked disappointed.

Meanwhile, Zeral chuckled quietly. He stopped himself, patting my shoulder with a serious expression. "In exchange, I'll count on you lending your ear now and then when something happens with Feris. Or...you know...being my human shield."

"I refuse to be a human shield, but I suppose I can give you a shoulder to cry on."

The two of us shook hands firmly. *Negotiations complete, I guess.* Taking Noela along, Zeral and I walked toward an area I seldom visited on the outskirts of Kalta.

We eventually came upon a field full of wheat and all kinds of vegetables. *It's way bigger than I expected. Wow.* In a corner of that huge field was a meadow that looked as if it hadn't been used for some time; that was the one Zeral was letting me occupy.

"All right," I told Noela. "Let's get to planting these seeds."

"Plant, plant!"

Zeral said he was going to look around, and he left us to our sowing.

FERTILE SOIL: Perfect for agriculture.

According to my identification skill, it was fine to plant the seeds without modifying the soil.

As soon as I began doing so, I heard an unfamiliar electronic sound—the sort you wouldn't expect in this world. *Don't tell me...*

> SKILLS: Identification, Medicine Making,
> <NEW> Cultivation Ace (keeps crops from withering).

Whoa, I acquired a new skill! And a useful one to boot! In that case, I should sow as many seeds as I can. Cultivation Ace seemed to guarantee that none of the herbs would wilt, so I decided I should treat it as a support skill.

After I planted all the seeds I had on me, Zeral returned. "All done, Reiji?"

"Yeah," I replied. "I'll come back tomorrow to see how things look. Hrm...something wrong?"

"Well, crops here have been damaged at an alarming rate recently. I don't know whether we're dealing with wild dogs, wolves, or what."

Wolves? Oh...now that he mentions it, there were *claw marks on the field wall.*

"Why look at Noela, Master?"

"If crops are being damaged, the herbs we're growing might get messed up, too."

"Noela no eat without permission. No eat, Master." She shook her head.

I didn't know whether the culprit would eat our seedlings or not, but it sounded like the log walls surrounding the fields were no use at keeping anything out.

"Oh!" I exclaimed. "Right. I could use *that* on the field."

"You have an idea?" Zeral asked.

"Yup. When I come back tomorrow, I'll bring some good stuff along." I hurriedly headed back to the drugstore.

"What you make, Master? What you make?"

"Noela, you should probably wait outside the lab."

"Garoo?"

I uncorked a bottle of freshly picked utsubo flower petals.

"Arooo!"

Noela's fur stood on end and she dashed out of the laboratory. *Yup, the utsubo's working as usual.*

I heard Noela's voice behind me. "That no good, Master. Smelly. No good."

"That's the whole point."

To humans, utsubo flowers smelled like nothing, but they were incredibly potent to beasts and monsters.

Working briskly, I heard a voice outside. "Oh, my. What's the matter, Noela?"

"Grrr...Master stinky. No good."

"Gosh! You need to make sure to bathe, Mr. Reiji," Mina called. "Noela can smell it when you don't!"

I rolled my eyes at the misunderstanding. "C'mon, Noela. Explain to her what I'm doing, please."

I'd have to clear this up with Mina later. For now, I bottled and shook the ingredients, completing the process.

REPELLENT: Releases potent aroma that beasts/monsters hate.

A few days later, I put a hand above my eyes and peered about thirty meters ahead. "Oh, wow. This stuff works great!"

A black dog—likely the culprit behind the destroyed crops—lay on its back, its legs twitching. The repellent's aroma was so potent, the dog had just conked out.

Next to me, Zeral looked on. "What'd you do, Mr. Reiji?" he asked, befuddled. "What happened to that dog?"

I showed Zeral the repellent I'd made. "I spread this on the field wall."

"Oh—the treatment you said you were gonna make? What does it do?"

"It produces a smell beasts and monsters can't handle."

"You sure are fast with this stuff."

"I guess. Anyway, we won't have to worry about wild animals sneaking into the fields now."

I handed Zeral the bottle, and he happily spread the repellent all over the field walls. As we'd seen earlier, it worked perfectly.

The only problem was Noela. "Hate you, Master," she'd said earlier. Frankly, I was still reeling from the shock.

The process I'd used to make the repellent lessened its effects slightly. Still, the smell was enough to upset Noela, so I'd say it was effective.

Another wild dog approached. "Yo, Zeral. Looks like we got a guest."

"Oh, you're right. Let's see one more time just how effective this repellent of yours is."

The dog casually trotted toward the field. Then, about thirty meters from the wall, it stopped in its tracks and growled. "Garrrroooo..."

Suddenly, the wind shifted, blowing toward the dog.

"Arrrrrooo..." It collapsed and fainted. *Thump*.

The breeze must've carried the awful smell with it. "Perfect. It worked."

"R-Reiji! This is a simple magical barrier—something only mages can create! You made a gosh-darn barrier!"

"No, I made an animal repellent."

"It's all the same, as far as I'm concerned," retorted Zeral. "That repellent's a symbol of our friendship!"

"Could you please stop saying that stuff? It's embarrassing."

"Why?!"

"What do you mean, 'why?!'"

"It looks like I owe you yet again," he continued. "How much does the repellent cost?"

"Nothing. Let's just call it a complimentary service."

"C'mon, Reiji. Don't be shy. Call it what it is—*friendship*!"

"That's *not* what it is! You let me use your meadow, right? Providing the repellent is my way of thanking you."

"Aw. How boring," Zeral said, disappointed. Then he looked at my face and laughed a little.

By the way, the wild dogs were still alive and totally fine. They eventually woke up and fled.

I ended up selling the repellent for a pretty low price; it became a big hit among farmers dealing with wild animals. The only issue was that Noela refused to come anywhere near me when I made the stuff.

"Noela? Little Miss Noeeelaaa. Look, this is my job. I'm not doing it because I enjoy—"

"Aaarrrooo!" The more I inched toward her, the farther backward she pounced.

My tender heart can't take this.

"Have you still not bathed, Mr. Reiji?" Mina frowned.

"I have! I was just making a product with a smell Noela hates."

"Are you sure that you're cleaning the hard-to-reach spots? I'd be happy to wash your back for you."

"Jeez. It's fine. That'd be way too embarrassing."

Mina suddenly realized something. "Aaaaah! I completely forgot that you're male!" She clung to the ceiling.

"Yo—wait a second! What do you mean, you 'forgot'?! That's a problem in and of itself, Mina!" *We're such close friends that she doesn't even consider me a man?!*

She covered her bright red face with her hands. "Oh gosh, oh gosh, oh gosh…"

"W-well, it's okay. But just so you know…I'm bathing, you don't have to wash my back, and also, I'm a guy!"

And, like that, another (fun?) day passed.

15

The Drills Cometh Again

"**W**HY DRILLS HERE?"

"Oh, my. Good day, Noela. Is Sir Reiji in?"

"Master not here."

I'm in the lab, Noela. Despite that, I continued working. I guessed that the lord's daughter, Elaine, had come to play. As always, Noela made it clear she couldn't stand her.

"I've come with important business for Sir Reiji. When will he be back?"

"Day after next," Noela replied.

Hey. C'mon now. You know I'm in the lab.

"About what time?"

"Don't know."

At that point, I couldn't let the conversation continue. I popped into the drugstore. "I'm right here, Noela."

"Sir Reiji!" Elaine exclaimed. "I didn't know you were in. Good day."

"Uh, yeah. Good day to you too," I returned her greeting.

Noela trotted over and took my hand. Elaine's eyes widened. "You two sure are...close."

"Yeah, I guess. So, what's up? Here to chat?"

She shook her head. "Father's given me permission!" she said, her eyes shining.

Pardon? "Permission for what?"

"To work here!"

"Shouldn't you ask *my* permission for that?"

Noela nodded fervently.

"My father, the lord of this land, will let me work at Kirio Drugs for two whole days," Elaine continued. "He says it'll be a good opportunity to learn the ways of the world."

"Why didn't anyone ask me whether it was all right?"

"Hmm? *Father* said it was all right."

I struck Elaine's head lightly. *Thonk!*

"Owie! Wh-what was that for?!"

"Is your old man God or something?"

"As I said, he's the lord of this land!"

"That's not what I'm asking. I'm asking you whether being lord means everything he says is law!"

"Of course it does. Surely you know that much."

Argh! This is why Drills drives me up the wall. She can only think about things from her noble perspective.

"Why drugstore, Drills?" Noela demanded.

"Huh? B-because I know Sir Reiji."

"If only want to know way of world, other stores. Zing!"

I don't think I've ever heard someone say "zing" out loud before.

Noela sniffed the air, continuing her investigation. "Perfume. Drills wearing perfume."

"Oh, you're right," I agreed. "It's the charm perfume from the other day."

"A-and what's wrong with that?"

"Drills used for Master. Motive not pure. No need for work. Zing!" Noela jabbed a finger at Elaine.

"Is that a no, Sir Reiji...?" Elaine asked plaintively.

"Now, now. I think this is a grand idea," I told Noela. "We can have Drills help out around the drugstore while teaching her a thing or two about the real world."

That said, I wasn't sure I had specific work for Elaine to do.

"Understood," Noela said, much to my surprise. "Noela teach Drills."

"Yikes," I laughed. "*You're* gonna teach a young lady, Noela?"

"No longer Noela. Now Professor Noela."

She seemed gung-ho about putting the young aristocrat through the wringer. *Man, she really gets prickly when it comes to Elaine.*

Professor Noela immediately began her lessons. "First, werewolf different from beastling."

That's where she starts? Really?

"Um, I'd prefer that Sir Reiji taught me about work," Elaine objected.

"Master busy. No time deal with you."

Dang. Noela shoots straight. Will these two get along okay?

I headed back into the house, worried, and found Mina peeking into the drugstore with a big smile.

"You're in high spirits."

"Of course," Mina grinned. "After all, Noela's going out of her way to be friendly, despite her first impression of Miss Drills."

Would you describe this as "being friendly"? In the store, Noela explained various products to Elaine, one after another. From this perspective, Drills and the werewolf girl certainly seemed like they could be companions.

"It'd be great if they actually connected," I mused.

"Wouldn't it? Noela doesn't really go out of her way to associate with people around here. It'd be nice if she had a friend or two."

Just then, Mikoto trotted into the drugstore.

Noela greeted her immediately. "Yo! Welcome!"

At what point had that little troublemaker started saying "yo" to customers?

"Sup, Noela?!"

"Hrmph." Elaine took her usual haughty pose. "You did well bringing yourself here!"

Noela shook her head. "Wrong greeting, Drills. When customer arrive: 'Yo, welcome!'"

That's also wrong, actually. Could you please not *teach her that?*

Elaine cleared her throat. "Yo! Welcome!"

She legit said it. Why is she only cooperative when it comes to stuff like this?

"Now then," she added, "what do you want? I suppose I'll wait on you today, as a special favor."

Mikoto looked askance at both counter girls before putting two and two together. "Um, I'll take three energy potions, please."

"Oh, my! How dare you make an aristocrat like myself fetch items for you—a lowly commoner! You lack respect!"

You're *the disrespectful one!* I resisted the urge to head out there and make Elaine eat humble pie. At the end of the day, it was Professor Noela's job to correct that attitude of hers. *Hold it in, Reiji. Hold it in.*

I glanced toward Noela to see her reaction, only to spot her opening a bottle—the one potion I gave her daily—and downing it with shining eyes. *She really makes that stuff look delicious.*

Mikoto couldn't help laughing at the fact that Noela had already abandoned her duties.

At that point, unable to hold back, I rushed out and with a hand on each head, pushed them gently to bow in apology. "I'm really sorry my counter staff were so rude."

"Master, what wrong?"

"Wh-what's the big idea?!"

"Nah," said Mikoto cheerfully. "They're funny. It's all good."

Thank goodness they were dealing with her. I stuck around to make sure the two handled Mikoto's order properly before seeing her off.

"Listen up, Elaine," I snapped. "The customer's the customer. It doesn't matter whether they're aristocrats."

"But I'm nobility, and that girl was just a commoner! That was decided at birth; nothing changes it."

"Hi-ya!" I smacked Elaine's head fiercely.

"Owie! Y-you hit me again! Why must you be so hotheaded?!"

"Don't you dare patronize customers, Drills! Say *you* went to buy bread—"

"I'd never buy bread myself. That's a servant's job."

"It's an example. Whether you'd actually go is beside the point."

"All right. So?"

"Imagine if the bakery clerk was like, 'What do you want, bread? I suppose I'll get you some, as a special favor.' What would you think?"

"Hrmph. I'd tell Father immediately and have him shut down the bakery," Elaine replied casually.

"Argh! You entitled dummy! That's *exactly* how you just acted!"

Elaine thought for a moment before replying. "But she was a commoner, Sir Reiji. She possessed no power. Therefore, she could never destroy this drugstore."

"You idiotic noble! That's not what concerns me! Are you only capable of judging people based on how much power they wield?! If you keep acting like this, no customer in their right mind will come here, because you're awful. Got it, Lady Elaine?"

"U-um…could you say 'Lady Elaine' one more time? With passion…?" she asked, glancing upward.

"Uh, Lady Elaine…?" I repeated.

"Mm…I can imagine sneaking out of the mansion at night for a secret rendezvous. B-but it can never happen, since I'm a noble, and you're but a commoner."

Okay, yeah. Not really following. I turned to Noela. "And you! If Drills is gonna learn from you, you need to get your act together. No drinking potions in front of customers!"

"Grrr..." Noela's ears drooped sadly.

I lightly patted both girls' heads. "Everyone messes up. Just make sure to be more careful next time. Got it?"

"Noela try hard, Master," Noela replied. Her eyes burned with determination; her ears stood straight up.

Elaine nodded, clenching her fists childishly. "I-I'll try my best as well, even if I'm dealing with a commoner!"

Did she really need to add the "commoner" bit?

Since I was still kind of worried, I watched the store secretly from the doorway. Unsurprisingly, Elaine's huge attitude problem was still an issue. She constantly boasted about her household, tried to hard-sell products, and basically just acted as her usual snobbish self. My stomach sank the longer I watched her.

Meanwhile, Noela actually tried *too* hard, and didn't support Elaine at all. "Do it right, Drills!"

"I am!"

"No."

"I am! I absolutely am."

What kind of conversation is this? They're like a broken record. They say the more you quarrel, the closer you get— but is that actually true?

Teaching a noble girl the ways of the world was harder than I expected. The next day, I had Elaine help mix products instead of working inside the drugstore.

"W-we're all alone, Sir Reiji." Elaine blushed and fidgeted.

I showed no mercy and immediately put her to work. "Grab that. Next, that—no! Listen carefully, Drills. Yeah... Now crush it with that tool over there."

"This is completely different from what I expected when I imagined us one-on-one in the laboratory!" she complained, although she did exactly as I asked. "I was positive you were just making time for us to be alone together."

"Don't underestimate how tough pharmaceutical work is, you dang scatterbrain," I retorted.

After finishing a day's worth of products, we sat down to enjoy some tea Mina provided. Elaine looked at our surroundings. "Um...Sir Reiji? There's one more thing I'd like to make. Do you think it's possible?"

After asking her what exactly she meant, I agreed that it was a good idea.

I prepped the lab as I gave Elaine directions. I left most of the steps—cutting, crushing, kneading, squeezing— to her, but handled the final step, bottling and shaking the ingredients. If I didn't, my medicine-making skill wouldn't activate.

The next day, Elaine's internship ended, and a horse and carriage arrived to take her away.

"Thank you very much for the last two days." She curtsied politely and bowed her head to us. "I've learned quite a bit. Um...I'd like you to have something, Noela."

Elaine pulled out a bottle she'd been hiding and placed it in Noela's hand.

"Grrr...what this, Drills? Potion?"

"Ah ha ha ha! It's not a potion. Uncap it."

Noela did as Elaine instructed, and a wonderful fragrance greeted her.

"That's perfume," Mina remarked.

"Exactly." Elaine smiled shyly. "Um...I had Sir Reiji help me make a scent that'd suit you, Noela. I hope you like it."

Noela's nose twitched as she sniffed the bottle. "Smell good! Thanks, Drills."

Just like that, Elaine's concerned expression vanished. The whole time we'd worked on the perfume, she'd been terribly worried about whether Noela would like it. "Is it...all right if I come by again?"

"Uh-huh!"

"Thank you so much, Noela!" Elaine hugged the werewolf girl, smiling, and waved at us before leaving in her carriage.

"Isn't that great, Noela?"

"Arroo!"

Noela vanished into the back of the house, wagging her tail. Mina and I peeked and found her sniffing the perfume, closing the bottle when she got tired of it, then opening it again to smell it some more. She repeated this process over and over as Mina and I simply watched, smiling.

16

The Adventurers' Grief

THERE WASN'T MUCH BUSINESS at the drugstore today, so I kind of spaced out—only to hear footsteps approaching. I fought off a yawn and stretched.

A man with a poorly trimmed beard entered, calling in a loud voice, "Is the manager in?!"

He wore an old breastplate and gauntlets, and at his hip was a worn sword. He struck me as a veteran adventurer rather than a soldier. Outside the store were two individuals I presumed were his pals; all three men looked a little over forty.

"That'd be me," I answered. "How can I help you?"

The old adventurer introduced himself as Heath. "We'd like a hand with something, sir."

I had a bad feeling about that. The drugstore had

recently become something of a consultation service, with lots of people visiting to ask for vague help.

"What kind of help are we talking?"

"We heard that the Red Cat Brigade drove off several skilled bandits the other day. Apparently, they threw some kind of strange liquid at the bandits and captured them all alive—a strange liquid you created."

It seemed that this Heath fellow had heard about the capshin fluid. *Man, I really don't wanna make too much of that stuff. What if there's an accident while I'm mixing it? Not to mention that someone could misuse it.*

"I did in fact make that liquid," I replied. "But I don't manufacture the stuff except in extreme cases. If you're here to purchase some, I'll have to ask you to leave."

"No, you misunderstand! I'm not here because I want to buy it. A bastard of a kodola's appeared deep in the nearby forest. We took a quest to hunt the thing down, but we got our butts handed to us."

What the heck's a "kodola"? Some kind of monster?

Heath noticed my confusion. "Hmph. Sir, you don't know of kodolas? They're small dragons. About the size of two horses, give or take."

"Small dragons, huh?"

"That's why I'm here to request your help," Heath concluded.

This old adventurer sure wasn't acting like he'd *asked* me for help, more like my helping him was a forgone conclusion. *Ugh, what a pain. Why does it always have to be me?*

At the same time...the forest where this "kodola" thing had really popped up turned out to be the same one where Noela and I gathered herbs, which meant that until it was dealt with, we wouldn't be able to gather ingredients safely. Noela's search ability had kept us from encountering monsters up until now, but what if we had some bad luck?

"The thing spits fire, so it's pretty much impossible to get close to," Heath added, in a tone of voice like he was trying to show off his fighting experience.

I don't know who he's trying to impress here.

For now, I decided to find out the actual terms of Heath's quest. "Do you absolutely have to defeat this kodola thing?"

"It's an elimination quest. With that kodola running around, lumberjacks and hunters can't do their jobs in the woods—it breathes fire at them as soon as it sees them. It's a dangerous bastard."

I considered suggesting the animal repellent I'd made for Zeral, but I wasn't sure that'd be effective, since we were talking about protecting an entire forest. If I prescribed an inadequate repellent, the hunters would be in big trouble.

"Okay, I get the picture," I said. "I'll help, just give me some time."

"Mmm...hurry!"

Yeah, yeah. I had Heath wait in the drugstore and headed back into the house.

Noela was curled up on the sofa; I patted her back lightly. "Noela? Earth to Noela! Got a sec?"

"What wrong, Master...?" Noela rubbed her sleepy eyes as she sat up.

"Apparently, a dragon called a kodola turned up in that forest we always visit."

"Yup."

"Wait, you're familiar with the kodola? Has it been around for a while?"

"Mm-hmm. Kodola protect forest."

"Huh? Seriously?"

Noela nodded sleepily. According to her, the monster was fairly peaceful unless something endangered the forest. It usually forgave the presence of hunters.

"Well, it seems like folks in those woods are having a rough time," I explained. "I guess the kodola's been breathing fire."

"Kodola no fire. Very rare. See human, run away."

Noela explained that the kodola was a peaceful creature that didn't just attack humans on sight, even humans who came to strike it down. Once it sensed their presence, the kodola hid immediately. People rarely even saw the thing.

"Something's off," I muttered.

"Off?"

"Yeah. The lumberjacks and hunters put out an elimination quest on the kodola. They say the creature makes it too dangerous to do their jobs. But..."

"Weird. Kodola hide."

"Yeah. From what you're telling me, the thing's been in the woods for ages without anyone even knowing. Now, though, it's suddenly been spotted."

"No kill kodola. Endanger forest."

"Based on what you said, that's definitely not an option."

The werewolf girl stood up, suddenly driven. "Noela go check on kodola!"

Given her ability to search the forest for other creatures, I figured it should be fairly simple for her to find the kodola.

Ka-thunk! The door opened, and Mina entered.

"I heard everything," she said with a stern expression. "Let me pack you a lunch to take, Noela."

"Mina hurry-hurry."

"Hang on. Mr. Reiji, I'll make you a nice lunch, too."

Just like that, our little kodola-finding expedition started to feel more like a picnic. Heading back into the drugstore, I told Heath about Noela and her plan.

"If that beastling girl's telling the truth, then what happened to the kodola?"

"That's my question," I replied. "So, we're heading into the forest with Noela to investigate."

Noela wore a proud expression.

"Sorry for the wait!" Mina said, coming over with a basket.

Looks like she even packed enough lunch for the adventurers.

"I figured I ought to make you all some," she added. "I hope you enjoy it."

"Thanks for going out of your way," Heath said. "I'm borrowing your husband here for a bit, but don't worry, I'll make sure to get him back to you in one piece."

"O-oh, gosh! I'm not Mr. Reiji's wife," Mina cried. "I-I just live here, is all! L-Like a...uh...a freeloader!"

She escaped back into the house like a gust of wind.

"Ha ha ha! I'm jealous, good sir." Heath slapped my back hard several times.

Ouch, Heath.

"Shall we be on our way?" He marched forward, clearly in a good mood.

I guess Mina's homemade lunch cheered him up. That didn't take much, Mr. Adventurer.

The five of us made our way to the forest. Noela and I had last been here three days earlier. To be honest, nothing seemed particularly different. Noela transformed into a wolf and walked ahead, sniffing the air to detect other creatures' presences.

"Grrrrr..." Her ears and nose twitched, and she stopped in her tracks.

Directly ahead of Noela was a giant lizard, likely the kodola. It was large, with wide wings spread out on its back, and its mouth shot fire seemingly at random.

"See, good sir?" Heath frowned. "We can't get anywhere near the thing. Still, we're gonna take it down."

Don't get cocky.

KODOLA: Small dragon. Highly intelligent. Cowardly. Sometimes breathes fire defensively.

Noela had said that the kodola would hide if it recognized humans, which probably meant it hadn't noticed us yet.

"Hmm," I mused. "It doesn't really look as if it's trying

to attack us directly. But that doesn't change the fact that we can't get close."

"Wait and see. Lunch, Master."

Without my even noticing, Noela had transformed back into a human, reached into the picnic basket, pulled out the sheet, and spread it on the ground. Plopping down, she took a sandwich from the basket and chomped away.

"Arrroooo!"

Well, doesn't she sound happy? I wish I could be that carefree.

Since the kodola hadn't noticed us, we kept our distance and ate lunch. Even the adventurers sat down with Noela to eat, but I could feel a dark mood fall over the three of them.

"You're real danged lucky, you know?" Heath said. "A young drugstore manager gets to live in that house with a cute girl...!"

"She's good at cooking, to boot," added another adventurer. "You even have a beastling girl calling you master."

"You're a talented pharmacist, too. I'm so darn jealous."

I did my best to ignore the envy from the middle-aged adventurers. "What do you think, Noela?"

"Kodola weird. Close, should notice us."

What's up with it, then? The creature just sat there, breathing fire. The vegetation near the kodola was burnt, but the flames hadn't spread, fortunately for the forest. Still, if the dragon kept it up, there was no telling what could happen.

If the kodola burns down the forest, it'll get even harder for Noela and I to replenish our stockpiled herbs. We can't kill the thing, either.

Perhaps calming down, the kodola ceased breathing fire and ate some grass. It moved its large jaws up and down, then roared into the air.

"Master!" Noela exclaimed. "Master, kodola no eat grass. Animal carcass or tree nut only!"

"Wait, really?" Now that I looked carefully, I'd actually never seen grass like that before.

ARIMANA GRASS: Antipyretic medicinal herb. Effective against stomach pain. May be addictive/hallucinogenic in excess.

The kodola shouldn't eat grass—yet here it is, eating grass. And, according to my identification skill, consuming too much arimana grass makes you see things. I get it now.

"Basically, it can't distinguish between the real world and what's happening in its brain," I muttered. *Is it hallucinating some sort of enemy?*

"Master understand problem?"

"Yeah, I think so. The kodola's just a little confused, is all. If we fix that, it should go back to normal." *I just need to mix an antidote.*

I quickly explained the situation to the adventurers.

"This antidote of yours will cure the creature?" Heath asked.

"Yup. I'll go get what I need to create it. Think you guys can lend me a hand?"

"If we do, can I see Miss Mina?"

"Quit it," I snapped. "We're not that kind of shop."

"I-In that case, what about another homemade lunch?"

"We're not *that* kind of shop either. Give me a break."

"Th-then we refuse to help!" Heath cried.

Is this guy a child?! You're *the ones who couldn't complete this quest to begin with!*

"Would it really hurt you to share Mina's gentle, healing goodness?" Heath fell to his hands and knees, sobbing. "If she isn't your wife, can't I at least visit her? Can't she at least make me lunch?"

Man, fine. I gently patted Heath's shoulder. "I don't mind if you come to the drugstore as a customer."

"Thank you, good sir!" Heath cried with a worshipful gaze.

I swear, this guy's impossible. I haven't told him that there's a good chance I'll *be the one watching the store, but whatever.*

"Then you're gonna help?" I asked.

"Of course!"

Just like that, the past-his-prime adventurer was behaving again. Before long, we acquired the necessary ingredients for the antidote, and I rode Noela home so I could create the kodola's treatment.

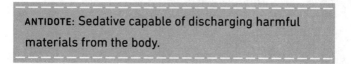

ANTIDOTE: Sedative capable of discharging harmful materials from the body.

With the new medication completed, Noela and I headed back into the forest.

Heath greeted us, smiling. "I'll bring some baked goods to the drugstore next time I drop in. Do you have any requests, good sir?"

"Er...why do you ask?"

"I just figured showing up empty-handed would be rude."

Now he's trying to get on my good side?

The old adventurer rubbed his hands together, a big smile on his face. "Does Lady Mina—er, I mean, Miss Mina—like sweets?"

"She sure does."

"Hmm, hmm." Heath nodded, smiling in what seemed

like a calculating way. "Hm, hm, hmm. Heh!"

His buddies looked exasperated. From their reactions, Heath was probably always like this.

"As I explained earlier, the antidote's in this little bottle," I reminded them. "Get the kodola to drink it."

When I tried to pass the bottle to an adventurer, they all averted their gaze. *They're like schoolkids who just got called on to answer a question.*

"Um, you gotta..." I trailed off.

"..."

"..."

"..."

Not a single one of them would look me in the eye. They put their hands in their pockets or behind their back, each clearly avoiding being the one to take the bottle.

This was your quest, not mine, you jerks! Why're you so against getting close to the kodola? Wasn't your quest to get rid of it? Where's your pride?!

Meanwhile, the kodola sat peacefully on the ground.

"Go forth, good sir," Heath whispered. "You know how to administer that antidote better than any of us."

His pals nodded in agreement. *I swear, these old dudes!*

"Argh, fine! I'll do it, okay?! But it's just because I don't want to lose my harvesting spot—and for the lumberjacks and hunters who use this forest, too!"

The old men applauded, impressed by my vigor. "Putting your nose to the grindstone is part of being young, good sir!" Heath exclaimed.

"Ha ha! I remember a time when I was just like you!" his companion added. "Takes me back. I used to think I could do anything and everything. Didn't even need sleep!"

"Heh! You're a real man, Sir Manager!"

"Shut up."

Noela tugged at my hem. "Ride on Noela, Master. Boosh glug glug."

Little Miss Noela, beyond "ride on me," I have no idea what you're trying to say. But I guess I'll do as you suggest.

She turned into a wolf, and I climbed up on her back. *I'm assuming that "boosh" of hers described the kodola breathing fire. And the "glug glug" was us making it drink the antidote...probably?*

Noela started to run. The kodola glared at us. *Eek, that thing's scary!*

The beast roared. "Groooaaaaaah!"

Noela completely ignored it and continued running. When the kodola's mouth opened, we'd both seen flames gathering in the back of its throat.

Now! I quickly tossed the small bottle I held into the

creature's mouth.

The kodola widened its eyes in surprise, swallowing loudly. *Yes! It drank the stuff!*

Noela stopped a fair distance away. I got off her back before she transformed into a human.

"Kodola acting different."

"Is it?" I couldn't see any change after the kodola swallowed the antidote, but Noela seemed to sense something.

The beast sat down again. "Groooaaah…"

That thing looks like it's in pain. Is it okay? According to my identification skill, the antidote shouldn't have negative effects.

"Well done, Sir Manager!" Heath raised his arms triumphantly.

Pssshhhhhhhhh…

With that uncomfortable noise, the kodola started to *pee*.

All over the old adventurers.

The beast kept going for nearly three full minutes, showering the middle-aged men, who were frozen in shock.

"…"

"…"

"…"

Having, uh…done its business…the kodola's expression

seemed relieved. "Grooaaah..."

"Master! Kodola feel better!"

"Yeah. Even I can tell."

The antidote is 'capable of discharging harmful materials,' eh? I guess it has a diuretic effect. Maybe it was a little too powerful.

But, hey, the kodola didn't look sick anymore; it seemed okay. A moment later, it noticed us and trotted away.

I'd call this a grand victory. From now on, if I see arimana grass, I gotta pick it all so this doesn't happen again.

After the horrifying shower, the three adventurers turned on each other.

"That's why I didn't wanna take this gig! Don't underestimate them monsters, dammit!"

"You dang wimp! You were the one who was all in! I told you this'd be a raw deal!"

"Well, I'd say meeting little Mina made this worthwhile," Heath concluded. "Harumph!"

"You gross old man! It's all 'Mina' this and 'Mina' that with you!"

"*Excuse* me?! Who are you calling a gross old man?!"

Ahh. Now, this is good. Keep at it! I chuckled, then turned to Noela. "Wonder why the kodola ate that arimana grass in the first place?"

"Don't know. Kodola eat meat and tree nut."

I searched quickly for the nuts Noela mentioned, but didn't find any. "Did the kodola maybe eat them all?"

"Nuts all on ground now. Usually in trees." Noela explained that the nuts grew in grapelike bunches. The kodola ate them off trees, but any it missed would eventually fall to the ground.

"So, the kodola ran out of food and ate the nuts off the ground, eating some grass along with them."

The three adventurers sprawled on the forest floor, exhausted.

"You weren't too bad."

"Heh! Because I'm stronger than you, of course."

"What the heck were we even doing on this quest...?"

That's my *question! You three thrust your quest on* me, *and then Heath decided to get a friggin' crush straight out of a high school soap opera!*

"Let's head home, Noela." Turning, I called to the adventurers. "We hope you'll return to Kirio Drugs!"

The three men responded with tired agreement. *They might have motivation issues, but they're not bad guys.* Leaving the forest, Noela and I made our way home.

Mina came out from the back and greeted us. "Welcome home, Mr. Reiji, Noela!"

"Mina. Master work *big*!"

"Oh, gosh! Is that so?"

Despite her clumsy wording, Noela successfully filled Mina in on the day's events.

To my surprise, tears welled up in Mina's eyes. She stared straight at me. "Um, Mina? Are you okay?"

"You aren't an adventurer, Mr. Reiji. You're a pharmacist! Why put yourself in such danger? When you're acting like this, how could I not worry about you? If anything happened to you, I don't know what I'd do!"

Now that I think about it, that was pretty crazy of me. "Hey, I'm sorry. I'll be more careful."

Mina kept crying, likely imagining the worst-case scenario. "Mr. Reiji, you're a pharmacist! You're not supposed to go on dangerous adventures!"

"H-hey, c'mon. Don't cry! I got home safe and sound, right?"

"Something happen to Master...Noela very sad." Just like that, Noela's eyes filled with tears, too. Clutching me, she began to weep in earnest. "Don't go, Master! Don't die!"

"You too, Noela?! Calm down! I'm right here. I'm not dead!" I stroked her back comfortingly.

Mina leaned against my chest as she sobbed. "Waaaaaaah! Mr. Reiji...!"

I wrapped my arms around them both, gently rubbing their heads. "I promise I won't do anything to worry you two anymore."

"Thank you...!"

"Noela protect Master!"

This was honestly a thousand times more effective than just getting lectured. *I didn't think they cared so much about me.*

The next morning, Heath visited the drugstore with dozens of baked goods.

"You really saved our butts yesterday, Sir Manager! Ha ha ha!"

He didn't wait long, did he? Kinda rude to show up so early...well, maybe those rules don't apply in this world.

This time, Heath wasn't in his adventurer's attire. He wore a formal-looking suit, and had a bouquet in one hand.

"Yeah, you're welcome," I replied. "What brings you here today...?"

"Is Mina in?"

I'd actually had her watching the store up until a moment ago, but Noela had sensed Heath approaching, so I took over for Mina. She'd told me yesterday that she felt uncomfortable with how Heath looked at her. He'd arrived just as Mina and I switched places. In fact, Noela and Mina were peeking into the drugstore from the doorway.

"Oh, she's doing chores today, I think," I told Heath.

"Is that so? Then could you give her these?" Heath placed the flowers and sweets on the counter. "Good day! If I ever need your help again, I'll be back."

"We're not consultants, so don't!"

I doubted that he was listening, since he simply laughed warmly and left. Considering how upbeat he was, you'd never guess that a dragon peed on him yesterday. In his shoes, I'd have curled up in a ball for days, incapable of setting foot outside.

The door to the back of the house opened, and Mina and Noela came into the drugstore.

"Wow!" Mina exclaimed. "More snacks? I'm so happy!"

"Mina, have you ever been described as 'easy to please'?"

"Huh? What do you mean?"

"Oh, nothing," I said. "I guess, even if you don't like someone, it never hurts to get flowers or sweets from them."

Noela had already dug into the treats, dropping the box with reckless abandon.

"Well, the flowers and sweets didn't do anything wrong." Mina smiled brightly. "Ah—but if you ever bought me something, I'd be happy with it no matter what it was, Mr. Reiji!"

Like I said, she's super easy to please.

Chuckling, I glanced out the window just in time to

see a dark shadow pass over.

Flap! Flap! Flap!

As that sound grew distant, I exited the drugstore and saw the kodola from yesterday flying away.

"Master! Master, look."

Turning to Noela, I found a huge pile of red nuts sitting on a leaf.

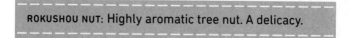

ROKUSHOU NUT: Highly aromatic tree nut. A delicacy.

Did the kodola come here just to deliver these rokushou nuts to us?

I couldn't really know what an animal like the kodola was thinking. Nonetheless, I yelled "Thank you!" to the dragon as it flew into the distance.

17

The Magic Sauce

T HE HOUSE WAS low on food, so I decided to eat lunch out. Noela and I made our way to the Rabbit Tavern, where we'd delivered the dish-soap prototype the other day.

As soon as we entered, the barmaid Rena greeted us. "Welcome, Mr. Pharmacist, Li'l Wolf!" Noela nodded, seeming happy that Rena used the nickname that the drugstore customers had started calling her.

Hrm...wait a second. It's midday, but we're the only people here. It's not like the Rabbit Tavern's always packed, but it's rarely this empty.

When Rena came by our table, I gave her our order. "Quiet today, huh?"

"Ah...ha ha ha...! More like *recently*."

"Really? It's been like this for a while?"

Rena grimaced and nodded. "It's that new restaurant—Combdale, I think it's called. They supposedly have some extremely delicious meat dishes on the menu."

On my way to the Rabbit Tavern, I'd picked up the pleasant scent of cooking meat. *I guess that must've come from the new joint.*

Noela began to drool, seemingly remembering Combdale's aroma as well. *What a handful.* I took out my handkerchief and wiped her mouth.

"So, Combdale's made it tough for you guys?"

"Exactly. They get even busier at night. More and more folks go there just to drink."

In other words, Combdale was competing in the exact same niche as the Rabbit Tavern.

"Dad's down in the dumps these days," Rena added. I noticed him hunched over the counter, looking completely downtrodden.

"Rabbit Tavern food tasty!"

I also liked the food here quite a bit. The Rabbit Tavern's menu might've seemed a little plain compared to the decadent meat over at Combdale, but it was consistent and delicious.

"Thanks, Li'l Wolf," replied Rena. "It's not like we're getting zero business. I'm sure we'll be fine."

So she said, but even I could tell that Rena was down.

"Combdale's owner came by once. He wanted to buy the whole tavern from us. Of course, Dad refused. When he left, the guy said he'd make sure we regretted turning down his offer." Unable to hold back tears any longer, Rena started to cry freely. "I just...I... What're we supposed to do? Th-the Rabbit Tavern's always been here! We could *never* sell it. What would we even do without it?"

"Grrr! Rena feel better!" Noela gently stroked the barmaid's head.

Rena hugged the werewolf girl tightly in return. "Thanks, Li'l Wolf."

Probably sensing that something was wrong with his daughter, the owner approached us. He looked to be in his late thirties, and he was as big as a bear.

"Sorry, Mr. Pharmacist. Looks like my daughter let the cat out of the bag."

"Don't apologize," I replied. "It seems like you guys are in a tough spot."

He let out a pained laugh. "Combdale's main location is in the capital, you see. They're going to towns all over, opening new spots."

"Which is why they're in Kalta...?"

"Yeah. Thing is, they never used to serve booze."

Selling alcohol at only this location was clearly a move to crush their competition. *I get it, business is business, but this still seems shady.*

The front bell rang, and another guest came in.

"Welcome!" exclaimed Rena's father.

"My, oh, my. I see this place is as messy as ever."

The visitor had an impressive mustache; I'd definitely have nicknamed him something snooty like "Pierre."

"I can see why you have no customers," guy-I-thought-of-as-Pierre said bluntly.

The Rabbit Tavern's owner shot him a glare. "Why're you here? Trying to buy us out again?"

"No, not at all! That boat's long since sailed," Pierre replied. "I'm here on business. You see, despite what you may think of me, I find your cooking impressive. What would you say to working at Combdale?"

Obviously, if Rena's father went to work for Pierre, the Rabbit Tavern would be no more. *Okay, this guy's enjoying this way too much, with that conniving grin.* I was just an observer, and even I was getting pissed.

"There's no point in sticking with a restaurant that won't last, right?" Pierre added.

"It's not just about profit," Rena's father replied. "I've poured my everything into this place. I won't shutter it so easily. Get outta here."

Pierre chuckled. "You'll come to regret this, sir. 'If only I'd sold the tavern back then,' you'll say to yourself! It won't be long until you come begging me to hire you. Until then, good luck." Pierre waved and exited the Rabbit Tavern.

"Do you have a plan, Dad...?"

The owner sighed and hung his head.

I totally understand, man. I own Kirio Drugs, after all. If someone told me to sell my store, I knew for a fact that I wouldn't agree. It wasn't about the cash. The drugstore was Noela and Mina's home, and it was full of all kinds of memories I'd shared with the townsfolk.

"Is there nothing you can do, Mr. Pharmacist...?" Rena asked.

"Grrr...Noela ask too, Master."

Both girls looked up at me.

"I really like this place, you know," I reassured them. "I don't want it to go out of business."

Still, at the end of the day, food was totally out of my wheelhouse. *Combdale uses meat's delicious scent to lure people in. I get why it's tempting.*

"Wait," I said to myself. "Meat's *scent*...?"

It was said that a human's sense of taste was more closely tied to smell than any other sense. Meat and grease smelled great, but it wasn't like you wanted to smell them constantly, or eat the same thing every day.

"I wonder..."

"Mr. Pharmacist, do you have an idea?" inquired Rena.

"I do. Just the other day, I got my hands on a bunch of rokushou nuts. Think you could use them?"

"Where'd you get such a gourmet ingredient? Rokushou nuts take a long time to prepare. They're typically used to make sauces, but even with the right ingredients, if you don't know the recipe..."

So, Rena's father can't make rokushou-nut sauce?

The older man let out a small sigh. "Although I do have a recipe, making the sauce without losing the nuts' flavor is really difficult."

I nodded, thinking. Ever since my little run-in with the kodola, the dragon dropped by once every three days to deliver rokushou nuts. They may have been a "gourmet ingredient," but I had plenty. We could afford to make mistakes. Plus, I had my medicine-making skill. To me, difficult recipes were nothing.

"In that case, leave it to me," I said. "Focus on coming up with a recipe to beat the new joint."

As soon as I left the Rabbit Tavern, Rena called out from behind me. "Didn't you drop in to have lunch, Mr. Pharmacist?"

"Look, I can do that later! I'll be back soon, I promise."

I turned around to see Noela with Rena, waving at me.

She clearly had no intention of tagging along. *She must really want lunch.*

I headed back home quickly, holing up in the laboratory so I could use the rokushou nuts. With my medicine-making skill—which honestly felt like cheating—I had no issue cooking the supposedly impossible-to-make sauce.

> **ROKUSHOU SAUCE:** Gourmet sauce made of rokushou nuts. Rich, unique aroma. Sour flavor. Refreshing aftertaste. Even the king himself rarely has a chance to enjoy it.

"All right. Now we can show Pierre what's what!"

◆Meanwhile, across town...◆

Kalta's new Combdale location was doing excellent business. Pierre—or, as he was actually called, Fernando—sat and counted his earnings from the restaurant. He thoughtfully stroked his curly mustache.

"If the numbers stay like this for the next few days, that cruddy little Rabbit Tavern doesn't stand a chance," he smiled. "Hee hee hee!"

Once the Rabbit Tavern closed, Combdale would be the only eatery left in town. When it came to villages in the middle of nowhere, there was never much competition, which made it easy to monopolize diners once other restaurants shuttered.

Earlier, Fernando had declared victory to the Rabbit Tavern's owner. He'd asked whether the man would like to work for Combdale, but he'd known full well that his rival would turn him down.

"I can just imagine him caving once things get a little bit worse for him," Fernando mused. "I wonder how he'll feel about coming to beg after turning me down once already. Hee hee hee...!"

However, things changed over the next few days. Curious about profits at Combdale's Kalta location, Fernando dropped in to see what was going on.

"Hrm. Business seems to have leveled off," Fernando remarked to the manager.

Combdale's manager could only respond with a shrug. They'd advertised in nearby towns, so there should have still been room for growth. At lunch, however, no guests had lined up. The nearly fifty empty seats inside Combdale's dining room stood out like a sore thumb.

Things like this were bound to happen occasionally, since people don't eat out every day—or that was how Fernando explained the situation in his head. But for the next three days, the number of guests dropped off sharply. Not just during the day, either, but also at night.

That, of course, meant that profits went down. What was going on?

For the first time since declaring victory over the Rabbit Tavern, Fernando decided to take a walk through Kalta. As he walked, he could made out some delicious aroma wafting through the air of the tiny, podunk town.

"W-wait. No way!"

There was no mistaking that smell. The rich scent resurrected memories deep inside him—memories of an incredible sauce he'd encountered at an aristocratic dinner party.

A famous chef belonging to the palace staff had made that sauce. He'd told no one its secret, and left no recipe behind before passing away. The king was said to have only a small amount stored, and he served it at only the most important occasions.

Handling rokushou nuts was exceptionally difficult. Even the most talented chefs were often incapable of preparing them without ruining their rich flavor. Whenever anyone attempted to make the royal chef's sauce, it wound up being a pale imitation or worse.

Fernando could tell that the aroma he inhaled was the real deal. "Wh-who made that sauce?!"

Following the scent's trail, he eventually reached a line of villagers in front of the tacky Rabbit Tavern.

"I-Impossible!" However many times Fernando rubbed his eyes, reality failed to change. Ignoring the line of villagers, he strode into the tavern.

The thirty-or-so seats inside were packed. The manager's daughter, along with the beast girl and young man who'd been there the other day, rushed around.

"Ah, if it ain't old Pierre," said the young man, a dirty plate in his hand. "If you want a bite, you gotta line up with the rest! You cut in front, right?"

"Urgh!"

Frowning, Fernando made his way to the back of the line. How had this happened? The Rabbit Tavern had been on the verge of closing, and yet now here it was, more alive than ever. It was his responsibility to learn exactly what had happened.

After a long wait, Fernando's turn finally arrived, and the manager's daughter guided him to his seat.

"We're not letting you speak rudely to us anymore," she cautioned him. "May I have your order, Mr. Pierre?"

"Who the hell is Pierre?" he retorted. "Er...you're serving rokushou sauce, right? Give me something with *that* on it."

The young woman nodded and turned around, giving the order to the manager behind the counter. The black-haired young man soon came out with Fernando's food. He set down a plate of steamed chicken, then poured on some light-red sauce.

"Sorry for the wait, Pierre."

"Again, who the bloody hell is Pierre?"

It didn't take the dish's aroma long to find its way into Fernando's nostrils. Unable to hold himself back, he swallowed loudly.

He'd caught its scent on his way to the Rabbit Tavern, but experiencing the rokushou sauce up close was entirely different. Its smell was an aromatic explosion.

Fernando stabbed a piece of chicken with his fork and took a bite. His nose filled with the rich scent. The sour tang of the sauce cooled the back of his tongue.

"Mm-mmm…" Fernando had never tasted steamed chicken this delicious in his entire life. His fork just wouldn't stop moving.

"Hey, Pierre. You're gonna choke if you keep shoveling it down that fast."

Rokushou sauce had another name. Because it went with pretty much any meal, people referred to it as the "magic sauce."

Before long, Fernando had torn through the chicken he'd ordered. Finally able to wrest his attention away from his plate, he looked at the diners around him.

Combdale's diners tended to be young men. Because they served meat dishes with greasy sauces to match, the food was heavy, and nobody really ate a whole lot there. However, the guests here at the Rabbit Tavern were of all demographics—young, old, men, women.

Thanks to the chicken's rich, sour flavor, they couldn't help wanting to eat as much as possible. The meal complemented alcohol perfectly; it even went well with bread. Plus, a single dish cost a measly five hundred rin. Selling rokushou sauce at that price was revolutionary.

"Wh-who cooked this rokushou...no, this *revolutionary* sauce? Nobody should be able to make it anymore! Was it you, Mr. Manager?!"

One glance told Fernando no. If the Rabbit Tavern's manager could make rokushou sauce this whole time, he would've served it a while ago. For the same reason, it was unlikely that the manager's daughter had anything to do with it.

That meant it had to be the young man who'd also been there the other day. "You're the one who cooked the rokushou nut sauce?"

"Hmm, I wonder," the young man shrugged.

"Well, let's strike a deal! I'll buy a single bottle of your revolutionary sauce for fifty thousand rin! How about that? Isn't that a great offer? Quite a price, right?"

"What's with you guys and the word 'revolutionary'?" the young man muttered. Grinning, he added, "Look, Pierre. I made this sauce for the Rabbit Tavern. If you want some, you're gonna have to ask the manager and his daughter. Hey, maybe if you grovel, they'll share it. Not everything in the world can be bought with cash, buddy."

Slam! Fernando smacked the table. "Damn it all!" He forced the rest of the meal down his throat.

"Delicious, right?" the barmaid asked Fernando as she collected the bill.

"Nnnggghhh!" Fernando threw the money at her and exited quickly, only to realize that he'd left his bag behind.

"Wait, Pierre!" The beast girl trotted out of the Rabbit Tavern with Fernando's bag. "Forget."

"Oh. Thanks for bringing it out."

His attempt to pat the charming beast girl's head was met with resistance. She slapped his hand away. "No touch, Pierre. Harassment!"

"You damn beastling!" Fernando remarked under his breath.

But apparently he wasn't quiet enough. "Noela not beastling!" she yelled while kicking him hard in the shin.

"Gah!" Fernando crouched in pain as the beastling fled the scene. "What did I do to deserve this...?"

This was all because that young man had made rokushou sauce. He'd said something about money not being the answer to everything, but that wasn't true. Everyone loved money—that was a simple fact.

Therefore, Fernando prepared a large sum of cash. It was one thing to say you'd pay fifty thousand rin, but it was something else entirely to offer someone the cash in person. To sweeten the deal a little, he added an extra thirty thousand rin on top.

Fernando waited in the shadows for the young man to leave, planning to negotiate after the tavern closed. He'd gone out of his way to prepare a backup plan as well. There was no way his strategy would fail.

"Heh heh! Once I get my hands on that sauce, the Rabbit Tavern will be no more!"

Soon, the black-haired young man left the restaurant.

"Greetings! Lunch truly was wonderful."

"Gah! Pierre's back," the young man mumbled. "What do you want?"

"About what we discussed earlier..." Fernando flashed his money bag. "How about it? A cool fifty thousand rin. I even have the cash here with me. What do you say to parting with a bottle of the sauce?"

The young man didn't appear remotely interested. He even yawned. "Didn't I tell you already? It's not for sale."

"Then what do you say to sixty thousand rin? Actually, no. Seventy thousand! Wait, make it eighty thousand!"

The young man's reaction didn't change, signaling to Fernando that now was the time for his trump card. Tossing the bag away, he smoothly transitioned to his hands and knees, bowing his head.

"Please, sell me the sauce! I beg you!"

"Ah, perfect timing!" The statement's meaning wasn't clear until the young man suddenly sat on Fernando's back, saying, "It's been a long day, and I'm tired. Been wanting a comfy chair to sit on."

"You're *sitting* on me?!"

Reiji stretched. "Didja say something?" he asked the living chair.

"Uh...no, of course not. So, um...how much do you want for the sauce?"

"I'd sell it for a million rin."

"A-a million?" In other words, the young man had no intention of parting with it. "Well, c-could you at least tell me where you got the rokushou nuts?"

"Oh, well, I'm friends with this great guy who drops in every morning to leave some. I give him a potion as thanks, and he just keeps coming back."

"At least introduce me to your friend!" Fernando begged, his forehead against the ground.

However, the young man's reply wasn't what he wanted to hear. "I mean, sure, but he's a literal monster. A really rare species, too. If you aren't careful, he might eat you."

Meeting a dead end, Fernando smacked the ground. "Damn it all!"

As long as the Rabbit Tavern had that sauce, it was game over for him.

The young man finally rose to his feet, looking down at the sobbing "chair."

"C'mon. Aren't you a grown man? Why're you crying? Look—I'll give you this, so cheer up, okay?"

Fernando took the bag. It didn't take him long to recognize, based on smell alone, what the gift was: steamed chicken in rokushou sauce.

"See ya." The young man left.

Fernando devoured the chicken. "Damn it... It's *so* good!"

Kalta's Combdale location had completely and utterly lost to the Rabbit Tavern and the young man's sauce. The chain's sales gradually declined, and they never managed to monopolize the market the way they'd hoped.

They had enough customers to stay open, but the Rabbit Tavern quickly took back the throne.

18

Nonstop Libido

ZERAL'S GIRLFRIEND Feris was requesting a treatment that, needless to say, gave me pause.

The rather hotheaded girl had quietly made her way into the drugstore and told me, "I want to have Zeral's child."

Yup.

Can't they just take a day off to go at it like the dummies they are? I initially thought. However, things weren't as simple as they seemed.

"Recently, Zeral hasn't really...well..." Feris looked uncomfortable. "He isn't interested in me."

So, Zeral's the problem? Maybe he has a girl on the side?

Feris was reportedly so very concerned that she hadn't been sleeping, which sounded like the same vicious cycle they'd been in before. Images of Feris running around with a knife raced through my mind.

So, Feris wanted a prescription that would get Zeral in the mood—something like a love potion. I told her to give me time to think about whether I could fulfill her request, and sent her home.

Soon, the man of the hour waltzed nonchalantly into the store. I hadn't heard anything from Zeral about another woman, so I interrogated him. "Uh, how're things going with Feris? Getting along? Any fighting?"

"Huh? Er, no fighting. Why?"

Hrm. I wondered whether I should tell Zeral that Feris had come by asking me for a prescription. *That'd technically be a breach of privacy, right? I should probably keep it to myself.*

"It's nothing. You thinking about marriage?"

"Marriage...? Pretty much. Feris is the daughter of a wealthy merchant family from the next town over, and our parents are fine with the idea."

At first, I'd thought Feris was after a shotgun wedding, but that didn't seem to be the case. She and Zeral were just genuinely celibate. Since they were practically engaged, I could see why she'd find that concerning. I questioned Zeral seriously, but it didn't seem like he was cheating.

"Is something going on, Reiji?"

"No. It's just... I think you should, you know, take things as they come. If you and Feris love each other, and you're both thinking about the future...I think it's okay to move forward, you know? Besides, you're rich."

"Er...what're you talking about?"

"Nothing. Nothing at all."

"Huh?" Zeral tilted his head, confused.

I could imagine someone being unable to, uh...get it up...if they were tired or just not in the mood. Maybe that was the issue?

As I pondered this, our conversation turned casual, and Zeral eventually went home.

I decided to fulfill Feris's request and make an aphrodisiac. I didn't want Feris to start swinging a knife around in public again, after all.

Noela and I headed into the usual forest together and gathered numerous herbs, including the roots of a plant called "muku." All that was left was to pick up some fruit from the marketplace to make the treatment more palatable.

"Welcome home, Mr. Reiji!" Mina had held down the fort in our absence. She'd apparently overhead some of my conversation with Feris earlier. "What sort of medicine will you be making today?"

How should I explain this? It's kind of awkward telling a young woman. "Er...medicine that energizes you, I guess."

"Energizes? How is it different from your energy potions?"

"Um...let's just say it's a little more targeted."

"Tasty-tasty? Energy tasty?" Noela seemed extra interested.

"Yeah, Noela, I'm gonna try my best to make sure it comes out tasty."

Managing to avoid the awkward details, I headed into the laboratory. As usual, I followed the directions my skill outlined, and I had no problem quickly whipping up the medication.

> EMOTIONAL DRIVE: Aphrodisiac. Strengthens emotions.

Er, is this really the right treatment? Especially considering its initials...

My skill called the new product an aphrodisiac, so I must've succeeded. Still, its description worried me a bit. *I could test it, but without a partner, it'd be kind of depressing...*

Okay, extremely depressing.

Since Zeral was swinging by tomorrow, I'd just give it to him and ask for the details later.

"All right," I muttered to myself. "Tomorrow night should work out just fine for them, then."

After using the washroom, I headed back to the

laboratory, only to find that the treatment I'd just made was missing.

"Huh? It's not here!" I searched the lab hastily. "Where is it? Where'd the aphrodisiac go?"

This is weird. I know for a fact that I left it right here...

I heard Mina's voice from the other room. "I might be a bit worn out from all the housework, Noela. My body just feels so heavy recently, no matter what I do."

"Master's new medicine. Energy flavor!"

My jaw dropped. *No, wait! Mina can't drink that!*

I rushed into the living room. Just as I feared, Noela had given Mina the medicine I'd crafted.

"Mina, don't!"

It was already too late; Mina gulped it down.

"Oh, I'm so sorry!" she cried. "Noela said it was an energy drink, so I couldn't help myself."

As she apologized, her cheeks flushed, and her eyes narrowed. She looked like she was about to topple over. Panicking, I caught her in my arms.

This treatment's initials are "E.D.," but that's coincidental. It's not like it's just for men.

"Wh-what should I do, M-Mr. Reiji?" Mina's eyes welled up as she gently rubbed her knees together. She turned bashfully away from me. "I'm...I'm feeling like a very, very lewd girl."

Well, that's direct! Come on, Mina. Saying something like that with that look on your face is super unfair.

I just wanted to pick her up like a princess, take her to the bedroom, and totally... *Er, obviously that's not going to happen. Wait—what about the antidote I gave the kodola the other day? It's supposed to calm you down!* I was pretty sure the drugstore had some in stock.

I set Mina on the sofa, only for her to wrap both arms around my neck and pull me close.

"Whoa!"

"Hee hee! Where do you think you're going, Mr. Reiji?"

"The store, Mina."

"Even though you did this to me?"

"I certainly didn't. The medicine did."

"Who *cares*?!" Mina kissed my cheek.

"Hey, c'mon, stop that! Don't blame me if you come to your senses and die of embarrassment later."

"I'm *already* dead!"

Gah! Now she plays the ghost card?

"You can totally ravish me if you'd like." She sounded enthusiastic about the idea.

"You'll regret saying that when you go back to normal."

"I've been dead a while; I've spent years regretting all kinds of things. Who cares if I add one more to the list?"

"This is getting heavy."

Noela watched Mina immobilize me, then aggressively nodded. "Mina full of energy. Energy very important."

She grabbed the rest of the E.D. treatment and hurried out of the living room.

"*Yo!* W-wait, Noela! *Noeeelaaa!*"

Closing the door behind her, she exited into the drugstore.

"Noela this, Noela that, Noela, Noela," snapped Mina. "You're always *so* focused on Noela. I wish you'd look at *me* more often!"

C'mon, Mina. Don't say that with such pleading eyes.

"If you don't, I'll haunt you! Hee hee!"

Talk about the cutest curse ever. I sighed. "I get it, I get it! I'll do whatever you want later, okay?"

I once again tried to head for the store, only for Mina to take my arm and tag along, giggling. "Mr. Reiji! Mr. Reeeiiiiji!"

All I know is that I need her to drink the antidote, and fast.

As I entered the store, I saw Noela with Annabelle. The Red Cat Brigade's captain held a bottle of the aphrodisiac.

"Energy tasty. Energy important," Noela informed her.

"Ooh, thanks, little lady! Lately, I've been pretty exhausted." Annabelle downed the bottle's contents in one go. *Gulp!*

"Ah!" I cried. "You can't—"

The captain dropped the empty bottle to the floor. *Clunk!*

Her intimidating expression changed, and her sharp gaze grew relaxed and come-hither. "What's happenin' to me, Pharmacist? I feel...weird."

Suddenly, Red Cat Brigade members gathered outside the drugstore, looking in. "I knew it!" one exclaimed.

"B-Boss?" another asked. "What's wrong?"

Annabelle looked up at me with an uncharacteristically confused expression. "Am I...really not attractive enough? I know I'm rough and tumble, but I...I'll work on that, I swear!"

The members of her brigade looked positively *smitten*.

"Our foul-mouthed, tough-as-nails boss is showin' her feminine side," one breathed. "Gah! She's so cute."

Shouldn't you guys be on patrol?

"Y'all need to get back to work, stat!" Annabelle ordered.

"You're the one who gets potions every morning, right?" Mina demanded. "Just to catch a glimpse of Mr. Reiji?"

"N-nuh-uh." Annabelle's voice was quiet. "I'm just... free in the morning, is all. It's a coincidence."

Mina puffed her chest out as if bragging. "After this, Mr. Reiji and I are doing all kinds of smutty things together."

"We are *so* not," I interjected.

"Mind if I join and we make it a three-way?" Annabelle asked.

"Ah!" Mina exclaimed. "What a delightful idea!"

"*I* certainly mind!" I snapped. "Don't get on board, Mina!"

The lecherous women to either side of me kept me pinned. I gazed at the drugstore shelf; I still had two antidotes left, thank goodness. *If I can just get them to drink some...*

"Noela! Grab the antidote off the shelf for me!"

"Understood. Leave to Noela, Master!"

She made her way to the shelf I pointed at, stretched her arm up as far as she could, and grabbed both bottles.

"Garrroo?"

But with a tinkle of broken glass, the antidotes slipped out of her hand and fell. The smashed bottles leaked their contents onto the floor.

I made eye contact with Noela, whose expression read as pure panic. "Noela."

"Remember important thing. Must do. Bye!"

"You *liar*!"

Noela immediately fled the scene of the crime with wolflike speed.

"Gaaaaah! Noeeelaaa! Come *back*!"

She did not, in fact, come back. The drugstore interior went quiet.

"Now then," I said. "I just recalled something *I* have to take care of, so I'll take my leave!"

Mina and Annabelle squeezed my arms tightly.

"Mr. Reiji."

"Pharmacist."

I ended up making more antidote with both women clinging to me. Then, somehow, I got them to drink it.

Let the record show that I'm extremely *exhausted.*

◆◆◆

The next day, Mina wriggled on the ceiling, covering her face with both hands. "Oh my gosh, what've I done?"

There was no point chiming in with an "I told you so," since I doubted Mina would remember that.

"I'm so embarrassed, I could just die," she cried. "I-I can't believe I kissed you. Waaah...!"

Annabelle, on the other hand, failed to pick up her daily potion order, instead sending a familiar Red Cat Brigade member to grab it. According to him, she wouldn't be showing her face around the drugstore for a while, so other members would handle the transaction from then on.

"I dunno what happened, but if anyone mentions what went down yesterday, she kicks their ass," he said before leaving. "You should be careful too, Medicine God."

Noela finally made her way home, apologizing for breaking the antidote bottles. I forgave her immediately.

Before long, a pathetic-sounding voice called out to me while I watched the store. "Reiji, buddy, listen to *this*!"

Zeral appeared. *There he is. Damn lovebird.*

"Before you start complaining, I have a prescription for you." I handed him the bottle, warning him to be sure to drink the energizing medicine with Feris.

"Huh? Is it dangerous?"

I sighed. "Why would I give you something dangerous?"

He sniffed it. "If this is basically an energy potion, no need to wait till I'm with Feris." Then he chugged the whole bottle. "Huh? My body feels all hot...!"

"Could you *please* listen to my directions?!" I force-fed him a bottled antidote immediately, then remade the medication and sent Zeral home with it.

Lucky for me, Feris never came back to follow up.

I'm just gonna assume the problem was solved.

Every time I saw the happy couple, I couldn't help thinking that they needed to hurry up and just tie the goddamn knot.

19

The Ghost Commits to Results

AFTER CLOSING the drugstore, I found myself relaxing in the living room.

I could hear Noela and Mina in the bathroom. "This has become something of a problem for me, Noela."

"Mina squishy. Not there before."

"Eek! Don't touch me!"

What the heck are they doing?

Noela hopped out of the bathroom, her hair still wet. She smelled like good soap. Mina followed her.

"Master?"

"Hm? What's up?"

"Mina get big."

"Uh..."

I peered at Mina, but she didn't seem any larger to me.

No matter how hard I stared, I found Noela's words hard to believe.

Mina tilted her head toward me, drying her hair with a towel. "Is something the matter, Mr. Reiji?"

"Why would you say something like that, Noela?"

"Here, Master. Look."

Drawing close to Mina, Noela quickly pulled the ghost's hem all the way up—completely revealing her panties, of course.

Swish! Mina hurriedly pulled her dress back down. "Wh-wh-what're you doing, Noela?!"

"Showing Master."

"Well, don't!"

"No show panties, Mina! Show squishy tummy."

"I don't want to show him that, either!"

Well, "squishy tummy" certainly helps explain, I mused.

"I know Noela's saying you gained weight, but I honestly don't think that," I told Mina.

"Really?" She flashed me an easygoing smile.

"No, Master! Mina hiding lots." Noela poked Mina's stomach.

Mina slumped. "She's right, unfortunately. I am hiding lots, Mr. Reiji."

Hunh. So, ghosts can gain weight? I suppose, if Mina can

give herself a physical body, it can change like anyone else's. "Does your spirit body gain weight?"

"No," Mina replied. "I'm guessing this is because I've spent much more time in my physical body."

"I'm not sure there's much you can do about it," I said. "You can't leave the house, and you don't exercise, so..."

Noela and I frequently hiked through the woods to gather ingredients, so neither of us lacked exercise.

"I want to lose weight, Mr. Reiji," Mina said with a serious expression. *How rare.*

"I see. So, you're going to diet, then? Good luck!" I patted her back encouragingly.

Mina fidgeted, pushing her index fingers together. "Um, Mr. Reiji? If you don't mind, could you, um, make a treatment for me? I'd certainly appreciate it." She looked up shyly, like she was checking my reaction.

Weight-loss meds, eh? My medicine-making skill could make something that'd help her drop pounds. But...

"What is it, Mr. Reiji?"

"When it comes to dieting, there's no such thing as a shortcut. You have to put in the work yourself."

Mina clenched her fists. "I-I know... But there isn't a woman in the world who doesn't dream of losing weight easily! Right, Noela?!"

"Noela no gain weight."

"Traitor!"

Fwoof. Fwoof. Noela's tail wagged victoriously.

Mina cleared her throat. "There are exceptions to the rule—like Noela—but most women suffer over this! I'm sure if you made weight-loss medication, they'd buy tons! I can be your guinea pig! I promise I'll take it, no matter what!"

Talk about getting fired up. "Fine, I get it. How can I say no after all that?"

"Yay! Thank you so much, Mr. Reiji! I'll wait up till you're done making it." Mina hugged me tightly, overcome with joy. The impatient Noela latched on to me too.

I gently smacked Mina's head. "Don't expect too much."

At the end of the day, it's up to her to do this. I hope she gets that.

I peeled the two girls off me and headed for the laboratory, but Mina trailed me. "I'm going to help!"

Noela scoffed. "Mina have work, right? Chores. Do those."

The werewolf girl came with me instead. Tired after her nice, warm bath, she flopped over my lap, lay down, and fell asleep. She gripped her tail, sleeping soundly.

"So much for helping out," I grinned, beginning my work.

I grabbed some herbs I'd dried ahead of time, boiled them, and wrung them out. All that was left was to add a floral or fruit flavor to make the remedy easier to drink.

Shake, shake!

And the process was complete.

"Perfect. It's done."

KUCHIKUN JUICE: Stimulates metabolism. Makes burning fat easier.

Mina would need to drink the kuchikun juice daily; I made about a week's worth.

I took a sip myself. "Not bad at all." The aroma was quite pleasant, and it tasted a lot like fruit juice.

Mina trotted in, excited. "Is it done?! Are you finished?! Yay!" She grabbed the bottle of kuchikun juice.

Talk about crazy-good timing. I bet she was watching from outside the whole time.

I explained how the kuchikun juice worked, though it didn't seem like much of my explanation actually reached Mina's brain.

"Just to be clear," I said, "you won't suddenly lose weight just by drinking this."

"I know, I know! I have to put the work in myself."

Downing the drink, she sighed through her nose, satisfied. "Now Noela won't squeeze my tummy anymore!"

Man, I really don't think Mina needs to lose any weight, but... I touched her stomach gently. *Yeah, it's soft.*

"Eek! Wh-what're you doing?!"

"My bad, my bad. Mina, do you really need to diet? Personally, I think having some meat on your bones is a good thing."

"It's not! Too much meat and I'll become a ceiling blimp."

Is that really what'd happen? I certainly preferred someone soft over someone bony and hard, but this was Mina's call.

◆●◆

After I made the kuchikun juice, Mina drank a bottle daily, as instructed. It was less a medicine and more a lifestyle product, so I imagined the effects would differ from person to person.

For the hell of it, I drank the juice too. It was a simple enough thing to try—and hey, the more people testing it, the better.

Throughout the week, I noticed that my body went through some small changes. It seemed like a little flab around my stomach vanished. The problem was that, since I had no scale, there was no way to confirm it.

I took my shirt off. "What do you think, Noela?"

Noela nodded. "Different. Master little thinner."

"R-really? For sure?"

"Juice amazing. Master worked hard." Noela patted me on the head for my effort.

It wasn't like I'd really aimed to lose weight, but it was still cool that it worked out that way. I'd never believed in all those products that said you could lose weight just by doing one thing or another. *But maybe I was wrong.*

The real question now was how it had worked for Mina.

"Hey, Mina, how's the kuchikun juice working for you? I lost a little weight."

"Really? Congratulations!" Mina beamed. "In that case, I'm sure I must've, too!"

Investigator Noela raised her index finger and poked at Mina's stomach.

"Well? Well?! How does it look, Noela?"

Noela hesitated.

"I just went through the week without really thinking about it," Mina added, "so I have no idea how much weight I lost!"

Noela shook her head quietly. "No difference."

Mina froze, expressionless. She blanched as if she'd been told she had three months left to live.

Noela kept poking Mina's stomach. "Squishy, squishy."

"*Nooo*! Why?! Even Mr. Reiji shed pounds! Why is it just *me* who didn't?!" Mina looked at me with tears in her eyes.

Hey, come on, now. No need to cry.

"The kuchikun juice was supposed to make me lose weight!"

"No, no. Like I told you, that's not what that juice does. It just *supports* your weight loss. Uh...wait." I hesitated. There was a shelf underneath the sink where we put snacks and treats customers gave us as thank-you gifts. "Did you...?"

Mina, you dummy! I bet she snacked all this time because she thought she'd lose weight anyway! I opened the cupboard doors, only to find that half of the ten-or-so snack boxes that should've been there were gone.

"Mina, you've been snacking like crazy, haven't you?"

"I-It's not just me! N-Noela's been snacking, too!"

Zoom! Just like that, Noela was gone. *I wasn't going to get angry at her, but I guess she thought otherwise.*

I turned to Mina. "Look, I'm not mad about the treats being gone. I'm upset that you snacked during your diet." Since she was always in the house, there was no way she'd lose weight if she ate like it was no biggie.

"I-I want to lose weight easily," Mina scowled.

"Dieting ain't that easy," I responded, although it wasn't like I knew enough about diets to make a blanket statement like that. "Mina, do you actually want to lose weight?"

"Of course I do!"

"Okay, then. Since you can't go outside, let's have you lift weights. And no more snacking."

"Ugh..."

"You aren't that halfhearted, are you? You're serious about dieting, right?!"

"Uh-huh! I-I'll do my best!"

I put together a light weightlifting schedule for Mina, and she began another week of drinking kuchikun juice. Needless to say, she didn't snack this time. Noela helped her exercise, and Mina made her way through what she described as a "stoic" week.

Investigator Noela once again poked Mina's stomach. "No more squishy-squishy."

"Mr. Reiji! Noela! I did it! I did it!"

Mina clasped our hands and spun around, clearly thrilled. And really, the changes I'd had her make weren't that severe—just cutting out snacking and lifting weights for about the same amount of time I usually exercised. That kuchikun juice really did work well.

"Thank you so much, Mr. Reiji!" Mina exclaimed. "It's all thanks to you and the juice you made!"

It was worth making that kuchikun juice if it meant seeing Mina so happy.

Sadly, tragedy struck only two weeks later.

"Mina squishy-squishy."

"Nooooo! *Again*?!"

She'd rebounded. *At the end of the day, it's all about committing to results.*

20

The Pharmacist and the Hunting Festival

FROM INSIDE THE DRUGSTORE, I smelled a delicious dinner cooking in the kitchen. I glanced outside; it was already basically nighttime.

I wonder what's for dinner today.

I started closing up quickly, eager to relax and eat... only for a young girl to come into the store just before I could lock up.

"Reiji?" It was the beautiful elf girl, Ririka, Kururu's little sister.

Kururu had evidently been quite busy lately; he hadn't dropped by the store in some time. On the other hand, Ririka popped up now and then.

"What's up?" I asked her, annoyed. "I'm closing."

She headed toward the counter. "No need to be so mean about it."

"If you're gonna visit, I'd appreciate it if you did it earlier."

"I have stuff going on during the day, all right?"

"So, what's the deal? Try to keep it short."

"There's going to be a hunting festival in the forest soon."

"A what?"

"Basically, an annual contest to see who can hunt the most monsters and animals. No magic's allowed, so the best archer wins."

Hrm...I see. I glanced at Ririka.

She blushed slightly. "My brother's an amazing archer, right? Every year, he ends up winning. This year, though, he's organizing things, so he won't compete. That means I'll be a contestant, but I'm not very good with a bow."

"Before you continue, let me set you straight—I can't create a medicine that'll make you good at archery."

"Th-that isn't why I'm here! Don't be rude." Seemingly hurt, Ririka turned away from me.

"What's the deal, then?"

"Can you...prescribe something that'll help me win, even though I'm a poor archer?" she asked quietly.

Is she kidding? That's an even more difficult request than "make me good at archery"! "Like hell!"

"B-but why not?! You prescribed my brother medicine that let him hit a bullseye every time! I know all about it!"

"I've never created anything like that," I replied. "All I did was make him some eye drops. They cleared his vision up a bit and made it easier to aim."

How is it that, almost every time I produce a medicine, people seem to misunderstand its core purpose?

"Have you ever considered having your beloved brother train you in archery?" I added. "There's no need to rely on medicine for this."

"My brother treats me like a child. 'Archery's too difficult for you,' he says over and over. So, I don't want to rely on him."

"You'd rather fix your problems with medicine, though?"

Ririka stared at the drugstore shelf silently, nodding without making eye contact.

"But what's the point of that kind of victory?" I asked. "I personally think that if you work hard at archery but lose anyway, there's nothing to be ashamed of."

"I want to show Kururu up! By winning the hunting festival, I'll prove to him that he was wrong to treat me like a child. I'll really impress him!"

Hrm. I crossed my arms. Ririka normally acted tough, but now that she'd showed her true feelings, I started seeing her side of things. She'd already done her best to improve, but nothing had worked. I was her last resort.

It might've been unfair to the other competitors, but at the end of the day, I wanted to help her out. It wasn't like there was a cash prize or anything for winning. To put it bluntly, all that came with victory were bragging rights and the nebulous concept of honor.

"All right, I get it," I said. "I'll help you."

"Really?"

"Yeah. But there's no way I can give you a prescription without knowing how good you are with a bow. I also can't create magic medicine that'll guarantee that you get first place or become a better archer. Got it? All I can make is something to help you along the way."

"I understand."

That was how I decided to help Ririka win the hunting festival.

◆◆◆

The next morning, Noela and I headed to the part of the forest where Ririka always trained.

"Morning, Reiji, Noela!"

"Good morning."

"G'morning."

After we exchanged greetings, Ririka pulled back her bowstring and released it.

Swoosh! The arrow flew past the target some twenty meters away, striking the mountain of sand behind it. She shot a second and third arrow. Neither hit the target.

"I-If you have something to say, just say it!" Ririka cried. "I-I know I stink."

"I didn't think anything like that," I replied. "Show me your hands."

She tried to hide her hands; I grabbed them. "Hey, wait, stop!"

I examined the painful-looking blisters all over Ririka's palms. *How will she concentrate on hitting her target when her hands are in such bad shape?*

"If it hurts, you should just say so."

"It's not like complaining's going to make me a better archer."

Jeez. She's so hardheaded.

I'd brought a bunch of potions and energy drinks for this very purpose. "Noela, grab me a potion."

"Grr?"

Noela was sitting on the picnic blanket we'd laid on the ground, being good. She was drinking the potion I gave her every morning; savoring it had become a favorite ritual of hers.

Noela passed me a bottle from my bag. I had Ririka drink it.

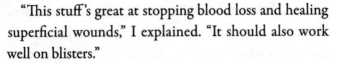
"This stuff's great at stopping blood loss and healing superficial wounds," I explained. "It should also work well on blisters."

"I didn't say my hands hurt."

"Just do me a favor and accept the act of kindness like a good girl." I stepped away.

Ririka resumed her training. Just like I'd expected, with less pain in her hands, about one in five arrows struck its mark. "Well, look at that. You can hit the target now."

"That's always been the case," Ririka retorted. "It's not like I missed every single shot."

Still, it was true that she wouldn't hit a monster running through a thick forest anytime soon.

Noela had apparently grown bored. She picked up Ririka's spare bow and a single arrow.

"You know how to use that thing?" I asked.

"No." Imitating Ririka, she pulled the bowstring back and fired an arrow. The projectile zoomed through the air and hit the bullseye.

"Aarrooo! Master! Hit! Hit!" Noela's tail swished back and forth.

"Whoa! Awesome, Noela!" I patted her head.

"H-how'd she hit it dead center so easily?!"

"Garrooo!" Noela held her head high. She shot yet another arrow, and once again struck the bullseye. "Garrooo! Bow fun, Master!"

The werewolf girl fired arrow after arrow. I saw the determination fading from Ririka's eyes as she watched the display.

"I think you're about to break that little elf's heart, Noela. Actually, it's already broken. You gotta stop."

"No, it's fine," Ririka sat down and held her knees sadly. "I'm just a worthless, talentless, garbage elf."

Here we go. I did my very best to cheer her up, finally persuading her to give training another shot. The next step was for Ririka to show me the distance she could guarantee a bullseye from.

"Huh? From there?" I winced.

"Y-yeah. Got a problem with that?"

She's literally five meters from the target! In a classroom, that'd be something like three desks. I didn't really have a problem with that, so much as I was shocked that Ririka thought she could win the competition.

No, calm down. You promised to help her. You gotta do something! Hm...it's not like wild beasts will just trot up close to her so she can hit them. And they certainly aren't gonna sit still. So, what can I do...?

"Ah!" I exclaimed. "That's it!"

"What is it?" she asked. "Did you figure something out?"

"I'd like you to practice with a short bow, Ririka."

She was holding a normal bow. If she could only hit targets from five meters away, however, she didn't need a long-range weapon.

"No way. Those're for kids."

"Are you in any position to argue, considering your skill level?"

"Ugh..." My strategy somehow got a reluctant okay from Ririka, despite her clear distaste for it.

I continued explaining my plan. "The idea is to raise your skill level with a short bow, so that you can always hit your mark within a few meters."

"And victory will be mine!"

We nodded to one another and immediately got to work. Ririka headed home to grab a short bow, and Consultant Noela and I talked over the materials necessary for her order. Then we gathered fruit, flower nectar, and tree sap.

We returned to the drugstore, and I was able to mix the exact product I'd been shooting for; even Noela gave it her seal of approval.

LURE: Scent attracts monsters/beasts. Very powerful.

Ririka's got this in the bag, I concluded.

♦Ririka's Side♦

On the day of the hunting festival, about fifty familiar elves gathered. Everyone from young elves to older veterans were present. Why did people have to get so excited over an event that came around every year?

Now and then, Ririka heard laughter as people saw her armed with a short bow despite her age. The fluid Reiji had given her was at her hip. *"Make sure you open the bottle in a clearing with good visibility,"* he'd advised. *"Then..."*

Ririka still hadn't used the lure herself, so her anxiousness was understandable. However, Noela gave the fluid her seal of approval, so the elf girl didn't doubt its effects.

In the distance, Ririka spotted her big brother Kururu waving.

"I'm going to show you what's what!" she muttered. "Just you watch!"

The start signal was given, and the elves all rushed through the forest at once. Their time limit was nightfall. Whoever took down the most creatures would be declared the victor; last year, Kururu managed to slay sixteen beasts on his own.

Ririka had to at least tie that number. She rushed through the woods, opening the bottled lure as soon as she arrived at a clearing.

Just like that, a wild dog appeared and advanced on her. "Garrooooo!"

"Whoa! I-It really worked?!" The wild dog's fierceness took Ririka aback.

Then she remembered Reiji's advice. *"Stay calm. Lure them in. Once they're within the range you practiced, let it rip."*

Now! she thought.

Swoomp! The arrow made a muffled sound as it flew a short distance and jabbed deep into the wild dog's flesh.

"I did it!" Ririka exclaimed. *One down.*

Just as she started to feel relieved, the other wild dogs came running.

"Garrroooo!"

"Arrroooo!"

"Garoorrroooo!"

"Grrroooo!"

Thump! Thump! Thump! Thump!

"Ungh…" Ririka grunted. "Stay calm. Lure them in. Once they're in range, let it rip!"

From her hunting spot, Ririka could see her surroundings clearly. There were boulders and large trees in the area. If her prey headed her way, they would thread down the narrowest path. That meant that, no matter what, the terrain would force them into a straight line.

Ririka fired another arrow from her short bow. *Swoomp!*

The wild dog in front collapsed. A moment later, Ririka's next arrow collided with the beast behind it.

"All you have to do is attract creatures with this lure, then draw your bow once they're in range. That's it," Reiji had explained. *"Don't go looking for them. Let them come to you. Nice and simple, right? As long as you have this lure, they should run directly at you. That'll make them easy to read and hit."*

Ririka shot the fourth and final wild dog, finally earning some time to catch her breath. "It's just like Reiji said. He's amazing."

Ririka remembered his joking words: *"Try not to get scared."*

She immediately responded aloud. "I'd never be scared of wild dogs!"

Rumble...rumble... It sounded like the ground itself was roaring.

Ririka narrowed her eyes. "What *is* that?"

Soon, the next creatures came into view, their paws slamming hard against the earth as they made their bloodthirsty way through the underbrush.

"Hmm...? *Huh*?! Th-there're so many! This 'lure' stuff works way too well!"

She'd chosen her spot well, though—even in those numbers, the wild dogs and small monsters were forced to approach her one at a time.

"Stay calm. Lure them in. Once they're in range, let it rip," she whispered, shooting repeatedly into the front of the pack.

◆◉◆

As for the results, Ririka came out on top of her debut hunting festival with a whopping eighty-nine kills. Every arrow found its target.

After receiving first place, she rushed into town to Kirio Drugs.

Ririka stopped for a moment and tilted her head. She'd competed to prove herself to her brother, yet the first person she wanted to tell about her victory wasn't Kururu. She'd heard Reiji's voice in her mind throughout the entire contest; he'd kept her going.

She wanted to tell Reiji that her win was all due to him and Kirio Drugs. Still, Ririka thought she might be too stubborn to get out an earnest "thank you." Even if she did, Reiji would probably just smile and say something like, "That's nice. Glad it worked."

Her heart aflutter, Ririka peeked into the drugstore. "Is Reiji in?"

There were no customers, and Reiji sat with Mina at the nearby counter.

"What shelf should this go on, Mr. Reiji?" Mina asked.

"Oh, that? Let's see."

"By the way, Noela was..." Ririka couldn't make out Mina's words.

"Ha ha ha! For real?" Reiji laughed.

They seemed to work together beautifully. For some reason, seeing that caused a sharp pain in Ririka's chest.

Zing, zing, zing!

There was a dull tinge to the pain that Ririka couldn't put her finger on. She felt as though she was watching something she shouldn't, yet seeing Reiji and Mina was nothing new. However much she thought it over, she couldn't figure the feeling out. Her knees locked, freezing her in place.

Noela was just arriving at the drugstore when she noticed the elf. "What wrong, Ririka?"

"Ah...um...I wanted to thank Reiji, and..."

"Master! Ririka here!"

Noela made her way inside to fetch Reiji; he answered her.

Suddenly, as if some kind of magic had been undone, Ririka's legs could move again. She'd come to see Reiji, yet now, she didn't want to. She found herself running through town, her chest aching.

"What am I going to do? I... I..."

I think I've fallen in love.

The Fleuret Family

I *WONDER HOW the hunting festival went.*

According to Noela, Ririka had in fact dropped by to thank me. By the time I came out to say hi, though, she was already gone. I assumed that she must've done pretty well—otherwise, I was pretty sure she would've come to tell me how badly I screwed up.

Anyhow, I was making medicine in the laboratory when Mina poked her head in. "Are you busy right now, Mr. Reiji?"

"Nah, not really. What's up?" *Did she gain weight again or something?*

"Ah!" Mina looked at me suspiciously. "I bet you just thought something very rude!"

"Nope! Definitely not!"

She came close and sat across from me. "Mr. Reiji, I...I want to go outside with you and Noela."

"I can't blame you," I replied. "I always have you watching the store for us."

I actually mulled over Mina's problem before. Was there anything I could do for her? Despite her physical form, she was still a ghost. I wasn't sure I could fix her ghost problems with my medicine-making skill.

"Have you ever *tried* going out?" I asked.

"Of course, although not for quite a while. When I put one foot outside the house, though, I'm immediately returned inside. I just suddenly appear back in the living room."

So, it wasn't like she was paralyzed outside, or ran into some invisible barrier. *She goes back to square one, over and over again.*

When we first met, Mina told me that if the people living in the house were truly happy, she'd be satisfied. I knew for a fact that I was quite happy with my current life, and so was Noela.

"Yet you're still here," I murmured. I'd originally thought that if she was satisfied, she'd move on to the next life, but she'd shown no sign of disappearing no matter how content we were. *What a mysterious ghost.*

"Is something the matter?" Mina asked.

"No. I just figure, if you could mess up and give me your panty-shopping list, it isn't impossible that you're wrong about going outside, too."

"J-jeez! Can you stop mentioning that list? Everyone makes mistakes! Gosh...you're so mean." Mina turned her gaze away, pouting.

Even someone as comforting as her can get angry sometimes, eh?

"Could you show me?" I asked. She glanced at me, signaling me to continue. "You know, the whole not-being-able-to-leave-the-house thing. I want to see how it works."

"All right. It happens really quickly, though."

She stood, walked toward the side door to the garden, and opened it. We made eye contact, and I nodded. Mina took a deep breath and stepped out of the house.

Just like that, she disappeared. I went into the living room to find her on the sofa.

"That happens every time," she sighed.

"Regardless of which body you're in?"

"Yes. Will I be stuck here forever?"

We repeated the disappearing process a number of times, but nothing changed. *I can't do much about this without knowing the cause.*

Mina sat on the sofa, hugging her knees. "I'm dead anyway, right? I'll probably never leave this house again. Ha ha...ah ha ha...!"

She really did wear her heart on her sleeve; that was one of Mina's charming qualities. However, in that position, she was giving me a full view up her skirt. *It's kind of hard to be serious when she's flashing me.*

"C'mon, cheer up," I smiled. "Who knows? You might suddenly be able to go outside again one day. And, hey, I want the three of us to go on vacation together. A company retreat! We can spend some of the money we've saved and really go all out. Sounds fun, right?"

Mina started to cry. "I...I'm so glad I met a homeowner as kind as you, Mr. Reiji!"

"There, there." I patted her head gently.

I'd comforted Mina, but even now, I had no clue what to do. *This might just be how ghosts work. If I try to force her out of the house, she could disappear forever.*

Noela heard us from the other room and trotted over. "Mina, what wrong?"

Mina hugged her tightly. "Noelaaa!" Cuddling the werewolf girl was enough to make her smile. I told you, that "fluffiness" stuff works.

"Why on sofa?" Noela tilted her head, clearly puzzled.

Mina didn't usually sit there. Normally, she was in the kitchen cleaning up, or going around tidying.

Actually, now that I think about it... I had Mina try to leave through different exits. Every time, though, she got sucked back into the house and ended up on the same spot on the sofa.

"Is something up with the couch?" I muttered. No, that couldn't be; I'd bought that thing when we moved in. "*Below* the couch, then?"

I looked underneath, but found nothing noteworthy; just regular flooring. But could there be something under the floor?

I looked at Mina, who was currently in heaven thanks to Noela's fluff. "Hey, Mina, did anyone ever renovate this room?"

"Actually, yes. The first family that moved in after I became the house guardian did some work."

She still calls herself a "house guardian," huh?

I didn't have the skill to rip up the floor, nor the tools. "Noela, get *him*."

"Him?! Understood! Go get now!"

Noela dashed out of the house. Ten minutes later, she returned carrying an old man piggyback.

It was Gaston, the carpenter who'd turned the house's

entrance into a storefront for us. As usual, he was hunched over at a practically ninety-degree angle. His mouth moved as he mumbled something or other; he looked like he might fall asleep at any second.

"See the floor under the couch, Gaston?" I asked. "I want to check what's beneath it. Can you make that happen?"

"Huh? What's that?"

Just like before, the guy could barely hear anything. "I want to look! Under! The *flooring*! Can you handle that?!"

"Ah, yeah! The old lady—right! Back in the day..."

I didn't ask about that.

"Right, right," Gaston continued. "In the end, he got cheated on!"

Again with this story? "*Who* got cheated on?!" I yelled.

"Under the flooring?" Gaston wheezed. "Sure, I can do that."

How did we get here? Damn it! I want to know how the story goes!

I didn't pry any further, though, since that had nothing to do with the problem at hand. Instead, Noela and I pushed the couch out of the way.

"Here, right?" Gaston rummaged through his toolbox. "Time to get busy!"

Pulling out some tools, he started to work; like before, he moved at a snail's pace.

"Um...how long will this *take*?!" I yelled.

"Let me see," Gaston mused. "I'd say about three days."

"That long? Okay, time to use the good stuff. Noela, can you grab some?"

Understanding my vague description, Noela brought a bottle from the drugstore. I offered it to the elderly carpenter.

"Here, Gaston. Drink this. It'll give you lots of energy. You might even work faster."

Gaston narrowed his eyes, inspecting the bottle. "What the heck's this stuff? Some kind of weird juice?" He'd completely forgotten that he'd drunk it before. Tilting his head, he took one sip, then two.

The bottle flew in my direction. I managed to catch it. *Take that! My number-two bestseller: energy potions!*

"You just hang onto your butt, lad!" Gaston exclaimed. "I'm exploding with energy! Bwa ha ha ha!"

He was like a totally different person, just as I'd hoped. *The Legendary Gaston has returned!*

The old man stood straight up, glowing with some mysterious aura. "This job won't take more than ten seconds! Gwaaaah! I can do it—I'm a legend! Ha ha ha!"

For the record, it took you longer than ten seconds to bark that out. Laugh maniacally as much as you want, but please, get to work. Of course, there was no way I'd actually say that out loud.

"I hope you don't regret awakening me," Gaston added.

"Why're you making it sound as if you're going into battle or something?" I scoffed. "I just hope you do a good job."

"Bwa ha ha ha ha!" Gaston laughed, and started to work with legendary speed.

Before long, there was a hole in the floor, allowing us to look below.

"As a bonus, take *this*!" the old man yelled, hinging a small trapdoor to the hole.

Fast, excellent work. Yeah, he really is a pro, I mused. *Despite the quality, he doesn't charge much, either. Talk about a good guy.*

"Call me the next time you need me!" Gaston exclaimed.

"Will do! Seriously, you're a real lifesaver."

After I thanked him, Gaston nodded and took his leave.

"What an amazing old gentleman," Mina marveled. "Is that what having multiple personalities is like?"

"Crazy. Very crazy," Noela echoed.

Oh, right. Neither of them have seen him in action. Gaston was quite a character—especially after an energy drink—so I understood their shock.

"Is there something below the floor, Mr. Reiji?" Mina inquired.

"If I'm right, something linked to *you* should be down there."

"Hunh." She didn't really seem to follow.

I wasted no time opening the small trapdoor; an old ladder led into the empty space below. I descended the ladder, but it didn't go far down. I reached the bottom in no time at all.

Near my landing spot, there was an old door, currently open. Beyond it, a room held a bookshelf, chair, and a desk; thick dust covered all the furniture.

Hrm...was I wrong? I thought something down here was grounding Mina inside the house, but...

I opened a desk drawer and discovered a petal-shaped brooch.

FLEURET FAMILY BROOCH: Expensive accessory set with green garnet.

Fleuret...? Now that I thought about it, I'd never learned Mina's surname.

"Mr. Reiji? Are you all right?"

"Yeah. I'm coming up now." I climbed back up the ladder and showed Mina the brooch. "Is this familiar?"

"Ah! I gave my mother this brooch to hold on to... Wow, the memories. It was in the basement?"

"Yeah. Why'd you give it to your mom?"

"It was something she gave *me* originally. She told me only to wear it on special occasions. I, um, didn't really have a chance to wear it at the time, so I had my mother hold on to it for me. In the end, I died without ever getting to put it on. Ah ha ha...!"

Is this what ties her to the house, then? It was time to check. Brooch in hand, I headed to the laboratory.

"Go outside now, Mina!" I yelled from afar.

Mina suddenly appeared in the air above and landed on top of me. "Eek!"

"Whoa!"

Thunk! My body broke her fall.

"A-are you okay, Mina?"

"Y-yes. Ah—I'm sorry!" She pulled away. "I didn't mean to land on you."

I rose to my feet. "Looks like we hit a bullseye. When you move a set distance from this brooch, it calls you back to its location."

To prove this theory, I had Mina wear the brooch, then step outside with me. Instead of reappearing inside the house, her feet landed on the ground outside like it was no big deal.

"I thought so! As long as you have this brooch on, you aren't tied to the house."

"Oh my gosh!" Mina raised both hands into the air. "I'm outside! I'm really outside! I can go shopping on my own! I can do anything! Mr. Reiji!"

"Yup! Now the three of us can go all kinds of places together."

Mina hugged me tightly.

"Whoa! Hey, now. We're outside, in public."

"I can go anywhere...! Waaaaah...!"

"Why the tears?"

"I'm just so happy!"

Noela apparently heard us from inside. She trotted out and clung to me as well. "Noela too!"

"Yo, Noela. Now that Mina can leave the house, how about the three of us go somewhere together?"

"Garroooo! Master, Noela, Mina, together!"

Noela's tail wagged enthusiastically back and forth—I could tell someone else was happy about this, too.

"A company retreat. We'll have to think about where to go," I added.

Mina rubbed the tears from her swollen eyes and smiled warmly. "Mr. Reiji, I'm the happiest girl in the world right now."

"Noela too! Noela too!"

"Yeah," I replied. "I'm pretty damn happy myself."

That was how Kirio Drugs' staff grew that much closer to each other.

Afterword

DRUGSTORE IN ANOTHER WORLD is a noveliza-
tion of a story of the same name, which I wrote
when I decided to become an author. It was published
as a large-format novel; this is the paperback version. I
even landed Matsuuni-sensei as the illustrator, making
this something of a new edition.

I must admit, this is my first time ever using different
illustrators for the same title, so it's a little mysterious
to me.

I'd be remiss if I didn't mention that the second volume of *Kou-2 ni Time Leap Shita Ore ga, Touji Suki datta
Sensei ni Kokutta Kekka* (*The End Result of Traveling Back
in Time to My Second Year of High School and Confessing
to My Beloved Sensei*) was released on April 15. It's quite
different from *Drugstore in Another World*, but I do hope

you give it a try. It's a romantic comedy about a man in his thirties who goes back in time to high school and dates the teacher he had a crush on.

If you're into romantic comedies like *Teasing Master Takagi-san*, I think you'll really like it! I recommend starting from Volume 1.

That's enough personal advertising! Now it's time to thank everyone who helped me out.

First, my editor. They were the only reason I could publish this story as a new edition. I even received the honor of being the first in their new novel lineup.

Then there's Matsuuni-sensei. I know our schedule was really tight, but I can't thank you enough for the adorable character designs you gave my heroines, and the lovely cover illustration!

I'd also like to express my gratitude to all the people involved in publishing this novel. You were a huge help!

Last but not least, thanks to everyone who bought this book. (Those of you in the bookstore, reading this afterword early, feel free to take it to the cash register!)

I'll keep giving this "writing" thing everything I have, so I hope you stay with me! Thank you so much!

—KENNOJI

FROM THE AUTHOR
Kennoji

I was making a point of going running four or five times a week, but during the winter, I skipped a bunch of jogs and gained a lot of weight...a whole lot of weight (too bad). Please, someone, make me some weight-loss medicine!